thousand returned to France. They departed from thence inexperienced conscripts; they came back well trained, warlike soldiers: and they took their place in the columns of the Grand Army. which was traversing France on its way to the Spanish Peninsula, to retrieve the disasters of the campaign.

Worley Publications

MEMOIRS OF GENERAL PÉPÉ

A facsimile reprint of the English edition of 1864.
Pages, 284.
3 Maps & Plans, 23 Illustrations.
Hardback (21.5 x 14cm).
Published 1999.
Price £22.00.
ISBN 1 869804 52 X.

General Gugliemo Pépé (1783-1855) entered military school in 1799 and was involved in the Neapolitan Insurrection at Ponte della Maddelena, and as a soldier in the Italian Legion in the Marengo Campaign. After some years in exile and captivity for his nationalist beliefs, he was promoted to Major (1806) under Massena, and as Colonel of the 8th Neapolitan Light Infantry (1811) under Suchet in Catalonia. He returned to Naples as General to command a Brigade in 1814 and again in the tragic 1815 Campaign under Murat.

OTHER TITLES AVAILABLE

Gordon, Alexander - Journal of a Cavalry Officer in the Corunna Campaign, 1808-09.
Cloth 1990 £16.00 ISBN 1 869804 16 3.

Kelly, W.H. - The Battle of Wavre and Grouchy's Retreat.
Cloth 1993 £18.00 ISBN 1 869804 30 9.

Foord, E. - Napoleon's Russian Campaign of 1812.
Cloth 1994 £27.00 ISBN 1869804 34 1.

Chambers, G.L., Lt.-Col. - Bussaco.
Cloth 1994 £22.00 ISBN 1 869804 35 X.

Ropes, John Codman - The Campaign of Waterloo.
Cloth 1995 £22.00. ISBN 1 869804 38 4.

Lord Burghersh - The Operations of Allied Armies in 1813 and 1814.
Cloth 1996 £25.00. ISBN 1 869804 41 4.

Moorsom, M.S. - History of the 52nd Regiment, 1755 - 1816.
Cloth 1996 £25.00. ISBN 1 869804 42 2.

Recollections of Marshal Macdonald.
Cloth 1996 £25.00. ISBN 1 869804 45 7.

Memoirs of Baron Larrey.
Cloth, 1997 £20.00. ISBN 1 869804 46 5.

Miot, M.J. - Memoirs of the French Expedition to Egypt.
Cloth, 1997 £20.00. ISBN 1 869804 47 3.

Espitalier, Albert - Napoleon and King Murat.
Cloth, 1998 £25.00. ISBN 1 869804 48 1.

Hooper, George - The Campaign of Sedan.
Cloth, 1998 £22.00, ISBN 1 869804 49 X.

Wood, Sir Evelyn - Cavalry in the Waterloo Campaign.
Cloth, 1998 £20.00. ISBN 1 869804 51 1.

Yonge, Charlotte M. - Memoirs of Colonel Bugeaud.
Cloth. 1998 £20.00. ISBN 1 869804 50 3.

To order your copy or for further information about these and future books, please write (or telephone) to:-
**Worley Publications & Booksellers, 10 Rectory Road East, Felling, Tyne and Wear, NE10 9DN
Telephone: (0191) 469 2414.**

"Nava's debut fiction novel crafts a powerful narrative...
Nava's writing is laced with vulnerability, never shying away from the raw... Maya grapples with survivor's guilt...isolation... Nava deftly spotlights her decision to transform those feelings... on a journey of self-discovery...
Nava presents this...striking a balance between fact and fiction as she weaves the harrowing truth of Black July and its aftermath into this emotional narrative of transformation and resilience. The novel's quick pacing keeps its audience engaged, and readers will find themselves immersed in Maya's journey as she...comes to recognize 'the nature of humans [and] the nature of the world...'"
—*BookLife Reviews*

"Compelling... Allie Nava's words shine... *July and Everything After* creates a riveting story of survival and growth made all the more powerful for its roots in the real world...
Its special blend of emotional-driven experience… —and *how* Maya digests, comes to understand, and avoids…traps in her own evolutionary process will give readers and book club discussion groups much food for thought.
Libraries and readers seeking a story of immigrant experience…and most of all, a delicately woven tale of healing will welcome *July and Everything After* for its hard-hitting inspections of one young woman's life before, during, and after a cataclysmic event that changed her life trajectory."
—*Midwest Book Review*

"This universal story explores…the ripple effects of…traumas to diaspora communities. As a young woman grapples with feelings of social isolation and shame, she learns that activism comes in many forms and that helping others is a path toward healing her own soul."
—*Avril Benoît, CEO of Doctors Without Borders*

"The book was well written (and a debut!)... This was a fantastic, quick read that was emotional and educational!"
—*Joanna, @joannasbookshelf*

"*July and Everything After* is a powerful tale of resilience, identity, and the relentless pursuit of justice set against the backdrop of one of Sri Lanka's darkest chapters... The author does an exceptional job of...bringing to light the atrocities committed...with unflinching clarity... The contrast between life in the U.S. and Sri Lanka, is sharply drawn, illustrating the stark disparities in safety, comfort, and freedom... had me in tears... a beautifully written story..."
—*Mathi, mowgliwithabook*

"This cover is beautiful, and the story that lays inside of it is as equally impressive... What struck me was her thoughts of wanting to appreciate things in this country that we take for granted... A great book to read if you are looking for a story of resilience... and I was impressed this was a debut!"
—*Karen, @books.cats.travel.food*

"I really enjoyed this author's writing style... it brought me right into the story."
—*Stephanie, @thebooknerdfox*

"Maya's journey is empowering and full of wisdom... The writing style is...easy to get into..."
—*Amber, @_readtowrite04_*

"This book *immediately* captured my attention and I felt an instant investment in the people of Sri Lanka (and Maya!). The character development was interesting and the topics of...healing ...and a life after suffering trauma were all well done."
—*Allie, @bayeringwithfreshmen*

"…behind fiction lies some truth, that is how an author can take something and make it powerful, in this case I cannot imagine how much more powerful this author could have made this story…"
   —*Nicole, @reading_with_nicole*

JULY AND EVERYTHING AFTER

a novel

ALLIE NAVA

July and Everything After
Copyright © 2024 by Allie Nava

All rights reserved. No part of this publication may be reproduced, distributed, or transmitted in any form or by any means, including photocopying, recording or other electronic or mechanical methods, without the prior written permission of the author, except in the case of brief quotations embodied in reviews and certain other non-commercial uses permitted by copyright law.

Without in any way limiting the author's [and publisher's] exclusive rights under copyright, any use of this publication to "train" generative artificial intelligence (AI) technologies to generate text is expressly prohibited. The author reserves all rights to license uses of this work for generative AI training and development of machine learning language models.

This is a work of fiction. Any characters, businesses, places, events or incidents are either the product of the author's imagination or are used fictitiously. Any resemblance to actual persons, living or dead, events or locales is entirely coincidental.

Printed in the United States of America
Hardcover ISBN: 978-1-965253-05-2
Paperback ISBN: 978-1-965253-06-9
Ebook ISBN: 978-1-965253-07-6
Library of Congress Control Number: 2024915918

DartFrog Plus is the hybrid publishing imprint of DartFrog Books, LLC.
301 S. McDowell St.
Suite 125-1625
Charlotte, NC 28204

www.DartFrogBooks.com

AUTHOR'S NOTE

You do not always plan to be a writer. Sometimes it is simply thrust upon you, when you realize you have something to say on behalf of others who cannot express the words themselves. Sometimes the voices are so urgent, you have no choice but to get out of their way.

July and Everything After is a work of fiction, set against the backdrop of a few real events across North America and South Asia, like Black July.

Any opinions expressed in the book are those of the characters, and should not be confused with the author's.

CONTENTS

Part One 1
    Fire 3
    America 5
    Camp 13

Part Two 27
    Instability 29
    Radio 37
    Dreams 41
    Desire 45
    Bicycle 49
    Cooties 55
    Hotline 63
    Glasses 73
    Alone 85
    Trust 93
    Stuck 103

Part Three 111
    Discovery 113
    Betrayal 125
    Light 137

Part Four 149
    The Will, The Spirit 151
    Heavy 175
    Monk 183

Part Five 189
    Perspective 191
    Because of War 197
    Him 209
    Letter 217

Acknowledgments 225

About the Author 227

To my family, and to those who innocently lost their lives in 1983, 1981, and 1977 in Sri Lanka.

PART ONE

"I do not dispute with the world; rather it is the world that disputes with me."
—The Buddha

FIRE

The subtle scent of hibiscus Maya associated with her grandmother's house in Jaffna drifted in through the open car window on the eve of her twenty-second birthday in late July of 1983. She was en route to a train station near the capital city of Colombo in her birth country, Sri Lanka. Though she was too absorbed in the book she was reading to look for the source, she smiled at the memories the scent evoked.

A sudden screech of brakes caused Maya to look up. There was a crowd of people blocking the road in front of them, and Maya's heart began pounding in her chest as the roar of the crowd swelled and she realized that several people in the crowd were carrying torches. This was no ordinary traffic jam.

Without warning, a wiry man in a sarong that was folded and tied at his waist reached into the car and dragged her grandmother's housekeeper out by her hair. Another hand reached in and seized Maya's arm. Maya pleaded with the man to leave her alone, but he tugged, his fingers digging into her flesh, until she was out of the car. She felt a sharp sting on her left cheek as a bony hand struck her, and then Maya fell to the pavement.

Her father, who'd been in the passenger seat, fell onto the ground next to her. "Daaad!" she cried, as a man straddled her father and pressed his head to the ground.

Their car was on fire now, flipped onto its side. The crowd, emboldened by the sight, roared. Red and orange flames danced in the air, and the acrid smoke choked Maya's nose and throat and stung her eyes.

As the men swooped in to strip her of her meager belongings, Maya felt hands grab her purse and jewelry, and even the book still clutched tight in her hand. She smelled the sweat on their bodies and the alcohol on their breath.

What was happening? The driver of their car and the man who'd pulled the housekeeper out were talking, the driver shaking his head from side to side.

Suddenly Maya's father jerked his head up. "Vik? Is that you?"

The man turned his head to glare at Maya's father, his eyes stone cold.

"What happened?" her father asked, but Vik told him to shut up and turned away.

As if prompted by some invisible cue, two of the men holding Maya and her father let go and grabbed the housekeeper. In a swift motion, they thrust her into the flames that had erupted from the car. Quickly the putrid stench of flesh burning over fire overtook Maya. The housekeeper screamed and covered her eyes with the end of her sari. Her wails rose in a crescendo and then stopped entirely as the flames overtook her.

The rest of the men turned and glared at Maya. A few of them waved their arms, as if to summon others. One of the men began unbuckling his pants, and Maya looked around frantically for an escape route, but she was surrounded.

AMERICA

Just weeks earlier, Maya had been home in America, celebrating her recent graduation from college and beginning her job search.

Maya and her family had moved several times, an experience that had felt to her like an unfair game of hopscotch where the chalk lines were always being erased. First they moved from Asia—Sri Lanka, where she was born—and then within the US, always to a slightly better place, but none that ever felt like home. Her father's life savings hadn't been worth much in America, but he was full of determination to make a new life for Maya and her brothers. Their first apartment was two tiny bedrooms with bare mattresses and little other furniture. The mattresses were a splurge, bought with what her father had managed to save in their first few months in America, and a definite improvement on the bare floor they'd initially slept on.

"Why are there no sheets, Appa?" Maya had asked, not understanding that sheets were an unaffordable luxury.

Maya's father had a job teaching biochemistry in a small and unremarkable college that he'd lined up with the help of the US embassy. A shortage of people qualified to fill technical and scientific jobs had allowed him to take advantage of Congress's act in 1965 to open up immigration, and Maya's father, a biochemist, had benefited from that effort. Much of his salary, which was paid by a small company with a philanthropic interest in the college, went back to Sri Lanka to help Maya's cousins pay for books and clothing.

"They have no one else to help them," Maya's father explained when she asked why he would not keep the money to buy furniture.

Maya's mother had died while giving birth to her twin brothers; or at least, that was what Maya had been told. Maya had very few memories of her mother, and her father rarely spoke of her.

"Your mother was an American scholar, Maya. You know that," he repeated in response to her questions. "She traveled to Sri Lanka to conduct research. We met by chance at the Jaffna library."

In her youth, Maya had been teased by her new American schoolmates, who had found her clothes, hand-me-downs from families her father knew, ridiculous.

"What is *that* you're wearing, Maya? You look like a clown in those old clothes! Clown! Clown! Clown!"

Occasionally Maya would put on a dress—a *frock* as her relatives in Sri Lanka called it—that had been stitched by her father's sister, but mostly she wore the castoffs of strangers.

As she grew older, books became Maya's salvation and respite from this strange new world. She would spend hours at the local library reading book after book so she could forget her own life for a while.

Sometimes Maya sat on the concrete steps outside her home with her neighbor, a girl with freckles and short, mousy brown hair who was two years her senior.

"Look at this, Maya," the girl would say, plucking weeds from their small, shared yard. "Let's pretend to cook these in this Styrofoam cup."

In the early days of her new life in America, this girl was Maya's only friend, but when she moved to Pennsylvania, that changed.

AMERICA

Kelsie and Maya became friends their sophomore year of high school. Kelsie's neighborhood, although just a few blocks from Maya's, was far more elegant, which Maya discovered the first time she accompanied Kelsie home for dinner. It was the first time she'd ever been in a house with a formal dining room, and also the first time she'd had tacos.

"Here, Maya. Watch me. You fill your taco shell with tomatoes and lettuce and cheese," Kelsie said, reaching for the bowls.

"So where are you from, Maya?" Kelsie's father asked.

"I live down the road, in the next neighborhood," she said.

"Oh, I meant where are your parents from?"

"I just...I live with my father. I mean we live with our father. I have twin brothers. We just have one parent," Maya said.

"Well, my mother was from Norway," Kelsie's mom said. "She immigrated here when she was young, but she died, so Kelsie never knew her. My father was Irish, but he's gone now, too."

"My other grandparents still live there, in Norway," Kelsie added.

"What's Norway like?" Maya asked.

"Oh, it's beautiful and green, with beautiful fjords," Kelsie's mom replied.

"That sounds very nice," Maya said. She had no idea what a fjord was.

"And there are also beautiful churches," Kelsie's mom continued.

Maya's father had taken her and her brothers to a church near the town of Somerset a few times, but the church there was far from beautiful. Having grown up with mixed parentage himself—a Hindu Sri Lankan father and a Christian English mother—Maya's father had never been a regular churchgoer. At times when they still lived there, Christians were discriminated against in Sri Lanka, and so her father's family sometimes held prayer services at home, but Maya didn't remember those. She'd gone to church a few times with her father's mother, Esther, but she'd never been in a church she'd call beautiful.

On the first day at her new high school, Maya had set out on foot, knowing she needed to get past the house with the vicious dog that was next to horrible Mr. Haggerty's house. Maya steeled herself and averted her eyes as she passed the gravel driveway of the house where the dog lived, but before she was safely past, there was a flash of movement and the dog was lunging at her, barking and snapping its jaws.

Maya dropped her book bag and flute case, crouched on the ground, raised her arms in a cross to defend herself, and screamed as she waited to feel the dog's teeth in her flesh. Thankfully, as if someone had flipped an electrical switch in the dog's brain, it came down on all fours, turned around, and retreated up the gravel driveway.

Maya thought her heart would pound out of her chest. She remained crouched on the ground for a minute, breathing heavily, before slowly standing up and looking around to see whether anyone else had witnessed what happened.

Mr. Haggerty was sweeping his driveway just a few feet away. He had not moved to help. As Maya walked by, she heard him mutter, "You people… Why don't you go back where you came from."

Other than the morning incident, Maya had managed to get through the first day at her new school relatively unscathed, and even returned to the school that evening for the activity fair. The hall was crowded by the time she arrived, and she had to weave in and out of clusters of students, all of whom seemed to already be friends, looking for an activity she might actually want to pursue.

"Hey, are you here to sign up with the school newspaper?" a voice asked as she hesitated in front of a table. "I'm Jeev, by the way."

"Maybe. I don't know," Maya said. She glanced at Jeev, who looked older than the other students and whose skin color was darker than her own. He reminded Maya of one of her cousins and extended family back in Sri Lanka.

Jeev stepped around the table to grab Maya's elbow. "We need more people," he said, pushing up against the side of her hip.

Maya jerked back in surprise.

At that moment, someone took the microphone at the front of the room to make announcements. She shushed Jeev and turned to hear the announcements, watching him warily out of the corner of her eye.

"Look, it's too noisy in here," Jeev said, leaning close to talk directly into her ear. "Why don't you come with me to a get-together after this? There'll be other people from school. We can talk there."

Maya took another step away from Jeev. She was torn between wanting to meet other people from school and not wanting to go anywhere with him. She reluctantly agreed to meet him at the party, knowing she would never be able to tell her father about it, but when she arrived at the address he'd given her, Jeev was drunk, slurring and pawing at her. Maya left quickly, and ducked behind whatever was closest when she saw him on campus after that.

The bright spot of high school, besides Kelsie, was Sister Lucy, a substitute teacher who taught English and composition. She often didn't wear her nun's habit, due to some controversy about religious garb in public schools, but it might have been better if she did, because her enormous bust threatened to escape her blouses whenever she laughed heartily or sang enthusiastically, which was often. Even better than her soprano with its natural vibrato, though, was the way Sister Lucy treated everyone equally and made an effort to speak to students after class or in the hallways. She spent a lot of time helping Maya understand English literature and English composition, something she really needed with all the pressure at home to get good grades, and she also encouraged Maya to find a way to volunteer, saying that helping others was the best way to take your mind off your own troubles. Sister Lucy's joy and her dedication to serving others was so contagious that both Maya and Kelsie began to volunteer at Sister Lucy's peer counseling and crisis hotline. That was where Maya was when a call came in that sounded suspiciously like Jeev.

"My father doesn't support me; that's my main problem," the caller said. "I'll never be good enough in his eyes."

"I'm so sorry to hear that." Maya didn't know what else to say. "Is there anyone else you can turn to?"

"Not really. My parents don't get along."

"What about friends? Anyone you can talk to?"

"Not unless you call my drinking buddies my friends."

"Do you drink often?"

The young man let out a sigh. "Every day. Several beers a day."

Maya had been trained on the basics of teen and adult alcoholism, but only barely. The hotline was in such desperate need for volunteers that they allowed high school students to answer the phones, but there was no time to train them for every type of call that might come in.

"Can I give you the number of a few doctors and the clinic nearby here?" Maya asked.

"I guess."

"I'll call the clinic and make an appointment for you. The clinic holds spots for people who call the hotline."

Maya knew that the volunteers were supposed to listen to the callers' desperate stories and then refer callers to professionals.

AMERICA

After that, they had no way of knowing if the callers kept the appointments or got the help they so desperately needed.

As Maya lay on the dusty ground next to her father in Sri Lanka, the horrific smell of the burned housekeeper poisoned the air around her. America felt a million miles away, but Maya's desperate thoughts took her there, and a random thought pushed into her terror-stricken brain: if only she had a hotline to call right now, some way of getting out of this hopeless moment...

CAMP

The heat from the fire was excruciating as the men lifted Maya from the ground. She glanced at the terrifying leer on the face of the man who was unbuckling his pants, her eyes darting for an escape route. There was nowhere to go, no way to break through the wall of men.

Suddenly a hand grabbed her, yanking Maya's arm and pulling her through the crowd. She was running, running as fast as she could, and her mind went blank, its only thought to keep running.

Then it was dark and they were near railroad tracks and Maya's father was handing his wristwatch to a stranger.

"Take my watch," he begged. "Please. I don't have anything else. Please help us."

The man took the watch. He said something to her father, but Maya could not hear it.

A sudden gust of wind caused a movement to her side and Maya jumped. There was another woman present, standing by the train tracks, her long hair and dress blowing in the wind. Before Maya could make out anything else, her father pulled her arm sharply and they were running again. First over the train tracks, where their feet hit the metal with sharp clangs, then on dirt, where pebbles crunched under their soles, then through grass, which muffled the sound of their footsteps.

After what seemed like an eternity of running, they arrived at a nondescript building. It was gray, box-like, rising from the dust and dirt in defiance of its natural surroundings.

Maya's father nodded to her, as if they had arrived where they needed to be.

"Shhhhh," he said, putting his fingers to his lips.

A tall man dressed in a shirt and trousers appeared outside the building, waving at them.

He put his finger to his lips as they approached, then opened the door and motioned them into the building. They followed him down the hallway until the man opened one of the many doors and beckoned them inside.

From the vestibule, Maya could see a barren kitchen with a small window to the right. To the left there was a slightly larger room, filled with an industrial-style couch, a few chairs, and worn side tables.

Maya's father was whispering with the man, who left for a moment and returned from the kitchen with a small brown bottle with a white cap that he handed to Maya's father. Her father quickly unscrewed the bottle cap and pulled something out.

He looked down at where Maya was clinging to his shirt like a child and placed a tablet in her mouth without asking.

"I'm sorry," he said. "You'll have to chew this tablet, quickly, and swallow it. There's no water."

The tablet was excruciatingly bitter, but Maya swallowed it.

The noise outside—yelling and chanting—was growing closer. Maya gasped as light suddenly filled the kitchen window.

The man walked over to the window and held up his hand behind his back, a sign that Maya and her father should stay away. He turned from the window abruptly and said that they needed to leave. There was a mob outside, armed with torches, sickles, and machetes, and it was getting closer.

Maya and her father followed the man back into the hallway. There was chaos near the door where members of the mob had already entered the building. Maya tried to make sense of what was happening. Three men were on their knees in the hallway, and Maya heard them pleading, followed by the gurgling of slit throats. People were jumping out of the lone window in the hallway. The man pulled on their sleeves and led Maya and her father in the opposite direction, to a staircase.

As they descended, Maya heard a voice, as clearly as if someone was speaking directly into her ear. The action around her seemed to fade away as the voice said, *People are being attacked. People are being killed. There will be more cruelty, and you are going to experience an extraordinary amount of pain now. But know that you can move beyond this...*

It was the voice of the philosophy professor Sister Lucy had introduced to her in high school.

The voice faded and was replaced by the chaos around her and Maya scrambled to follow her father down the stairs.

When they arrived at the bottom of the staircase, the man opened the door and crouched down to peer out. Then he stood up and looked back at Maya and her father.

"Quickly. Walk that way, about half a mile to a mile, and you will come to an empty building. They won't think of going there."

"Why do you assist us?" asked Maya's father. "I know you are no different from them," he said, pointing with his head toward the door.

"Because..." The man paused and looked down for a second, then lifted his head. His words shot out like rapid fire. "Bloody hell, we don't have time for this. I am in charge at this building, this hospital. I am responsible for people to live, not die."

"I'm half—" Maya's father started to say, but the man interrupted.

"My quarrel is not with you," he said. "I have not had to suffer like your people, all these decades."

Maya was surprised by "your people." How did he know they were Tamil?

"Go!" the man said. "They are coming."

"We are indebted," Maya's father said.

The man was nodding his head. "Quick, go now! You don't have time."

Maya and her father crept outside. Men were screaming and chanting nearby, and there were several thudding noises and then reverberations that Maya could feel in her feet and legs. They started walking as quickly as possible without running. Maya could not see anything on the dirt path and simply followed behind her father, his shirt still clutched in her fist.

When they arrived at another building, there was a man standing at the door, as if on guard. When he saw them, he waved and said, "Quickly. Inside here."

They entered through a rusty metal door and went into a large room with high ceilings, like a school gymnasium. People were talking in low mumbles in the room and a group of men, women, and children huddled on the floor in one corner, clutching their legs to their chests.

Maya was exhausted. Her short, bobbed hair was soaked with sweat, and she was hungry and thirsty. She walked to the corner with her father, but he pointed to a group of women.

"You're safer with the other women," he said. Then he turned and went back to confer with the man who'd let them in.

Maya's father and this new man were talking in low, hushed tones, but she made out the words "attack" and "kill" and "refugee camp" and "Oliver." It had been a long time since Maya had heard someone address her father by his given name.

She leaned towards them, trying to overhear.

"Why? What else can you tell me?" her father asked.

"There were attacks near the train station," the man said. "A mob singled out and attacked the passersby that were Tamil."

Maya's father listened, nodding, his hand on his forehead.

"The attack was brutal," the man continued. "They assaulted and robbed the people there."

"That is also what happened to us," her father said.

"Where did you come from?" the man asked.

"The hospital. We were going to the train station, going north to Jaffna to my mother's house, but we were stopped by mobs. We barely escaped and ended up at the hospital."

The man nodded. "They burned the station master's car," he said, "and threw some of the passersby into the fire."

"That is precisely what happened to us," Maya's father said. "They took everything we had, set the car on fire, and threw my mother's housekeeper… We ran as fast as we could."

"Did you see the police?" the man asked.

"No."

"At the train station, apparently the police came, but did nothing," the man said.

"What? Bloody hell," Maya's father said, throwing his arms up.

"Some people tried to escape into the waiting rooms, but they were attacked, as well," the man continued.

"And the police did nothing?"

The man shook his head. "As additional trains arrived, those passengers were attacked, too."

"The hospital was also attacked," Maya's father said, briefly covering his mouth with his hands. "We were there, we came from there," he said.

"We can't upset the people here," the man said. "They are already afraid. I don't know what I am going to say to them."

"You have to tell them what is happening. They have a right to know," Maya's father said.

The man raised his hands to his forehead. "It's just awful. The houses and shops set on fire, and more being attacked throughout the area and..." The man hesitated, biting his lip.

"What?" Maya's father asked.

"At least one other town was attacked," the man said. "Perhaps several more, and many other parts of Colombo."

"That's odd," Maya's father said.

Maya could no longer sit idly by. She walked to her father and said, "If multiple towns were attacked, then it had to have been coordinated. Pre-planned and premeditated!"

Maya's father looked up, surprised to see her standing there. Then he said, "I think that's right. It must have been coordinated somehow."

"It couldn't be a coincidence," Maya said. "It could *not* have happened in multiple locations unless it was coordinated. I read about voter rosters being used in the past."

"What are you saying about voter rosters?" the man whispered.

"It had to have been—don't you see?" Maya said. She had been thinking about the men who'd pulled her from the car. They'd been unshaven and reeked of alcohol, with coarse language and filthy clothes. Maya wondered if they'd been recruited to participate in the mob by whoever had organized the attacks. They may have even been rewarded for taking part.

The man began rubbing his temples. "So many people have been killed," he sighed.

Maya's stomach churned, and she felt a gagging sensation rising into her throat. She was thinking about what she had witnessed at their car earlier, how the men had intended to rape and kill her, and the putrid smell of burning flesh when the men threw her grandmother's housekeeper into the fire. She couldn't get the sound of the men pleading in the hallway of the hospital, then gurgling and choking as their throats were slit, out of her head.

Maya walked back over to the corner of the room with her

father. She needed to think about something else. They sat down against the wall and stared at each other.

"Sleep," her father said. "There is nothing we can do now."

"I can't," Maya said. "My shoulders and arms and jaw are aching."

"There is nothing here," her father said. "No medical supplies. We can only hope the pain will subside."

"What about what the man here said?"

"We need to wait right now."

"For what?" Maya asked.

"I don't know yet. He said this place is a refugee camp now," her father replied.

"Who was the man you called out to earlier today?" Maya asked. She'd been shocked to hear her father call out to one of the men in the savage mob as they were under attack. "The man you called Vik?"

Maya's father looked down at his lap. "He used to be a friend of my sister's."

"He's the Vik she told us about?" Maya said. "How could he do that to us?"

"I don't know." Maya's father seemed to be searching for words. "He's Sinhalese, part of the majority here. He always saw past differences, though. I don't know what changed."

"Did he know we would be here?"

Her father let out a long sigh. "I may have mentioned something to my sister. I don't know if they're still in contact or not."

"He was so violently angry. He seemed unhinged," Maya said, searching her father's face for confirmation.

"Yes." Maya's father was silent for a moment. "And to think he used to attend poetry readings with my sister…"

Maya exhaled loudly, trying to ease the nausea rising inside her.

"Do you think we will be able to go home?" she asked. "Back to grandmother's house? Back to the US?"

"I don't know," her father replied.

At that, Maya began to cry, but no tears came out. A sharp pain in her stomach moved up into her chest and the room spun. She was afraid she would vomit or pass out.

Her father must have noticed, because he reached out and placed his hand on her shoulder, something he typically never did with her.

Maya took a few deep breaths to dispel the pain, then looked at her father, at his wavy brown-black hair and slightly crinkled forehead. Somehow, despite the havoc around them, he had managed to maintain his composure throughout the day.

Every inch of Maya's body was sore, and her hair, only recently cut just above her shoulders, was sticking uncomfortably to her neck and face. She lifted her hair off her neck and fanned herself until the nausea subsided.

"What do you think we are waiting for?" she asked her father.

"I don't know. Maybe water, maybe transportation. The man said that all of the trains have stopped running and everything is shut down. There are still mobs in the streets killing people."

"This happened before, didn't it? In 1981 and even before that, in 1977?"

Her father stared at her for a moment, then said, "Yes, it does feel similar."

"Thousands of people randomly killed, businesses and places of worship destroyed," Maya said. "It's all happened here before, hasn't it?"

Her father sighed. "Yes. I thought things might have calmed down."

"Oh, and the burning of one of the largest libraries in Asia," Maya said. "I read about that, too."

"After more than ten years in the US, I guess I thought things would be different."

Maya couldn't think straight anymore. She leaned back against the wall and pulled her knees up to her chest and hugged them, trying to calm herself and take her mind off her physical pain.

#

In the days that followed, Maya could not break free of the looming darkness and uncertainty, the inability to know who to trust, the emotional exhaustion, the wondering when—or if—they might see family members and friends again. Each day had only one goal: to survive and make it to the next day, despite the lack of food, beds, clean water, or health care.

At times, some act of courage from the people around her would break Maya's malaise. She tried to focus on her father's unrelenting fortitude and his ability to tackle each day's problems one by one. She made it a point to talk to the others in the shelter, to discuss their options and plot their escape and try to stay confident that help would come or there would be a window of calm in which they could all exit.

Maya's own will to survive waxed and waned. She tried to banish the thoughts of their current dire circumstances, purge her memories of the gruesome things she had witnessed, take her mind off the stress of not knowing whether there would be water and food. She forced herself to think about her grandmother Esther's house in the north where she and her father had been heading, the yellow bungalow with creepers growing up the side and the dusty road in front of the house. The inconvenience of her grandmother's outdoor concrete bathing tub and dark wooden outhouse seemed so inconsequential now.

She thought about the smell of orange pekoe tea and mangoes that filled her grandmother's house, and her mouth watered. What she wouldn't give for a slice of juicy, fleshy mango or a cup of her grandmother's Ceylon tea now.

Maya let her mind roam back in time, first to her final year of college in the US and her happy anticipation of the trip to Sri Lanka, then further back, to the home they had moved into seven years earlier in Pennsylvania. Immediately after her college graduation, that was where Maya had returned to begin her job search; the neighborhood and her small bedroom comfortingly familiar and the opportunity to reconnect with Kelsie and Sister Lucy unmissable.

Maya thought about the last few summers, when she had trudged in and out of different towns for summer internships, and the trip to London she and her father and brothers had taken two summers before. Her father had scrimped and saved to afford the airplane tickets, determined to introduce Maya and her brothers to members of their distant family. Then she scrolled back further in time, to the trip she and her father and the twins had taken to the White House, where the tour guide had never even heard of Sri Lanka, even though the US had had relations with the country since 1948.

That was where Maya stopped, unwilling to allow her thoughts to travel any further, to the early days in America and the tiny, dilapidated apartment with no furniture and no friends.

Eventually Maya would drowse off to sleep, and then startle awake, wondering where her brothers were. She would remind herself that the boys had not been with them in the car; they had been left behind at her grandmother's house. Only then could Maya sleep again.

After several days in the shelter without much food or water, Maya was exhausted and her stomach was painfully distended. A nasty smell, of worry and confusion and sweat and urine, overwhelmed her senses.

Her father tried to soothe her, to comfort her, as Maya looked around and asked, for the hundredth time, "All this—for what?"

Her father just nodded, pursing his lips. Then he stood up, saying he needed to search for more water.

"Please," she beseeched her father. "Maybe there is something else I can do to help. I've been talking to the others. I have some ideas." She could see her father's hesitation. "If I do something to help, I will feel better," she said. "I can't just sit here and wait anymore."

Maya's father studied her face intently before nodding. She jumped to her feet and went with her father to find the man who had originally waved them inside the building.

"Oliver," the man said as Maya and her father approached. "Thank you for always helping me distribute water." He patted Maya's father on the shoulder, then turned to Maya. "How have you stayed so calm?"

Maya was surprised by the man's question. She might appear calm on the surface, but inside, she was in turmoil. But this man actually did seem calm, as if they were all at a garden party rather than a makeshift refuge from murderous mobs.

"Can you tell me, what is the news?" her father asked. "What is happening now?"

The man said that he had heard on the radio that the trains and buses might start running again. The mobs that were torching stores, breaking windows, raiding buildings, and killing had finally slowed down.

"Can we go anytime soon?" Maya asked, glancing between the man and her father.

She was met with silence.

"I know I'm only twenty-two," she said, "but I can help coordinate inside if needed."

"We need to wait until we can get word out to someone to send buses here," the man said.

Suddenly overwhelmed by their luck in having survived thus far, Maya teared up. "There but for the grace of God I go," she said.

"What's that?" the man asked.

Maya's father turned to look at her. "It's just a saying my mother taught her as a small child," her father explained.

The other man continued to stare.

"You know, because we have been lucky so far," Maya said, "perhaps saved by some forces out of our control…like in some religious Tamils songs."

"Ahh, okay," the man responded, bringing his hands together and clasping them as if in prayer, bobbing his head sideways.

Maya and her father returned to their seats. That was all they could do now. Maya kept her head down and tried to distract herself, and she must have fallen asleep, because when she raised her head again, the man at the door was lifting plastic bottles out of a box.

The man told Maya and her father that somehow word had gotten to the municipal authorities that there were people who needed water, which is why the bottles had appeared. Someone had sent word that the trains and buses were starting to run, too, and one bus would soon arrive at their building. It would be enough to take only a third of the people out. Anyone who wasn't on the first bus might have to wait hours, maybe another day or two, for more buses to arrive.

"Maya, we are likely to be separated. You may have to go first, without me," her father said, turning to her, grabbing her shoulders.

"I—I won't know..." Maya tried to quickly process what was going on around her, and then said, "Yes, the train station. I'll buy a ticket to grandmother's and wait for you there?"

"Yes, go north first. We must get your brothers. I think they will provide you with a ticket at no charge, under the circumstances, at least I hope so. It's imperative you travel out of here when the bus arrives."

"We need to get out of here. Back to the US," Maya said.

Her father nodded.

"What will you do?" Maya asked with some consternation. The thought of leaving her father behind made her feel sick.

"I'll have to wait for now, for the next bus. We need to get the children, and as many women as possible, out first. Do you understand Maya?" her father said firmly, tightening his grip on her shoulders.

When the first bus arrived, Maya boarded and found a seat by the window. She looked out at her father, whose clothes were now dirty and frayed, and whose skin had become noticeably blistered in exposed areas. His wavy hair was blowing uncontrollably in the wind. Maya waved reluctantly to him, unsure whether she would ever see him again.

As the other women and children boarded the bus, Maya thought back to one of the first conversations she and her father had with the man at the shelter door. He had acknowledged that the Tamils, Maya and her father's ethnic group and one of the minorities in Sri Lanka, had suffered for decades and been persecuted, Hindus and Christians alike. The country's one-language policy from earlier days had alienated the Tamils and limited their access to government jobs, while quotas limited their access to university education. Maya's own father had been denied a spot in medical school, despite his high scores on the required entrance exams. Decades of systemic oppression, abuse, and violence had led hundreds of other desperate families to flee, just like Maya's family had, forever torn from the country and the people they loved.

Maya leaned her head against the window of the bus and tried not to cry.

PART TWO

"Life is a challenge; we must take it."
—Mother Teresa

INSTABILITY

There was silence in the house for days after Maya, her father, and her brothers managed to get out of Sri Lanka and return to the US, to their humble abode in the leafy suburbs an hour from Pittsburgh, near the town of Somerset. It was the home where Maya had spent the latter part of the 1970s wrestling with adolescent high school insecurities, which were made even more challenging by her foreignness and lack of a living mother.

Their escape from Sri Lanka had happened in a blur, and for days after arriving back in the States, Maya was mute, unable to respond to any of her father's or brothers' simple inquiries. Her father and brothers continued to go through the rote mechanics of waking, eating, answering phone calls, and running errands, but Maya was plagued by nightmares in which she relived the same horrible events over and over, nightly occurrences that left her drenched in sweat and feeling haunted by the ordeal. They had been lucky to survive, lucky to escape, and lucky to make it back to the US, but thousands of others had died, and tens of thousands had been displaced or become homeless.

"I know we just got back to the US," her father said at the kitchen table one morning between sips of tea, "but I've been thinking about whether we can ever go back to Sri Lanka now."

Maya did not respond.

"Where are the boys, by the way?" her father asked, putting his teacup down. "I was supposed to take them out to buy new bats and gloves."

"Don't you remember? They went back to college early," Maya answered, interrupting the cyclical deep breaths she used to calm herself each day.

"It's just as well. I don't know if they would fully understand what I'm going to say." He paused. "I thought it was going to be safe for us to return at some point in the future…or at least for me to retire there. This just confirms that it may never be safe, maybe not in my lifetime." His hand went to his forehead as if a headache were coming on.

Maya couldn't stop thinking about the fact that her father had known one of their attackers. That man, Vik, made regular appearances in her nightmares.

"Did you tell your sister about Vik?" she asked.

Maya's father looked down and shook his head. "I don't know if I can shock her like that right now."

"But he'll keep hurting more people if we don't alert—"

"Maya, what can we do from here?" her father said, crossing his arms.

"How can you say that, without even trying? Maybe your sister can speak to him, get through to him somehow."

"We'll just be setting ourselves up for disappointment. There's no reasoning with people like that," Maya's father said, shaking his head.

"So we just give up?"

"It's like a wild goose chase. You can become your own enemy—"

Maya cut off her father before he could finish. "Dad, how can you say—"

"Oh, so I'm *dad* again? Whatever happened to *appa*?" Maya's father stood up from the table and began to pace.

"I haven't called you 'appa' since we moved to Pennsylvania. I'm grown up now. Listen, we can't just give up," Maya said, following her father's pacing form with her eyes.

Maya's father stopped, crossed his arms over his chest again, and sighed. "I know. I know. I suppose you're right."

"Can't we do something here? Tell someone what happened? Won't the news outlets be interested?"

Maya's father stopped and shook his head. "It's not that simple. They have other priorities."

"What about our representatives?" Maya asked. "In all my government classes, we talked about writing letters to our representatives. Should we appeal to them?"

"What would we tell them?"

"We should tell them what we witnessed, what we went through," she said. "The US is a big superpower. Can't the US do something?"

"I'm not sure the government would care. I don't even know whether the US has any real economic interests there."

"What do you mean? They must have some? I know I read about American investments there at some point," Maya said.

"You remember what I told you about the massacres in 1977 and 1981? And the book burning at the main library in Jaffna?" Maya's father probed.

"Yes," Maya said, sitting forward in her chair.

"Those massacres were not widely in the news here, but we learned of them through relatives and friends. Those attacks were pre-planned, and likely state-sponsored, with the intention of targeting the minorities," Maya's father said.

"So, that's like what had happened to us, right? And it's likely voter lists were used to target specific homes and neighborhoods?"

"Perhaps," her father responded.

"So wouldn't that mean the government was sanctioning the killing of ethnic and religious minorities?" Maya said, watching her father twiddling with the pen in his shirt pocket. "Wouldn't the US government care about that?"

"Amnesty International has issued reports documenting the torture and killings of minorities," her father said. "The anti-minority sentiment has been reported on by a few journalists for decades. But very few in the international community have ever cared."

"Nothing has been done?" Maya asked.

Her father shook his head. "The government has been putting one-sided news into the international community, and that's what the world hears. People don't know the truth. For goodness' sake, the president of Sri Lanka publicly stated earlier this summer that he needed to put pressure on the minorities, and that the majority would be happy if he starved them."

"Wow." Maya shook her head, trying to imagine the American president saying something like that to the press. "So where are you getting your information, then?"

"I have friends who give me information, who have access to international news services like the BBC."

Maya nodded.

"Apparently, the president of Sri Lanka said that after the most recent riots, he would ban uprisings by anyone he called 'separatists.'"

"Separatists? What does that even mean?"

"I don't like that word. Some people call them freedom fighters. He meant the people who have been defending the minorities against political, economic, and military transgressions. Of course, the president failed to mention anything about the government's role. He didn't even denounce the violence. But he did tell journalists that the riots appeared to have been well planned and that they intended to track down the organizers." He shook his head. "Ironic, isn't it?"

Maya sighed. "So that's what all of your phone calls these past few days have been about."

"Yes. It's very serious now. Some international groups are making the case that this is genocide. Some have concluded that the government sponsored the violent riots and attacks on minorities in prior decades, too. They are calling it pogroms."

"Enough, please. I don't think I can hear anymore right now," Maya said as a feeling of panic rose inside her again. She set aside the juice she'd been sipping and resumed her deep cyclical breaths, focusing on the peeling brown plastic laminate of the table and the fraying brown vinyl fabric of the chairs.

"I've been wondering if maybe we should move to where we have other relatives?" Maya's father said abruptly. "Maybe Canada?" He started pacing across the small kitchen floor again. "We know people there."

"But we're home now. Why move again? I thought we were settled here."

"You can search for jobs in a new country, can't you?"

"It's not that easy. I don't know if I can get into a foreign graduate school or get a job... It's hard enough here, where I'm a citizen," Maya said, rubbing her temples. "It would be more difficult for you, too. You have a good job here, and people you know, don't you?" Maya asked, wondering just how integrated her father felt at work. "You can't replicate that very easily somewhere else, right?"

Maya's father murmured and scratched his head. "You're probably right."

The suggestion to consider leaving the US was something Maya had heard too many times growing up. Her father's sister was in Canada, married to an engineer who managed projects for the government, and his mother was, of course, still in Sri Lanka, having resisted for decades the pressure from her own family to return to England. Maya had realized a few years ago how destabilizing it had been for her to always have the threat of starting over in one of those countries constantly looming overhead.

"We need to be here for the twins, anyway," she said. "They're in the middle of college. They can't just leave."

"I don't relish the idea of leaving, either. It's better here, especially for you. I know that," her father said, his tone softening. "I just wonder if we shouldn't be closer to family."

"Maybe I can do something to shine a light on what we witnessed this summer," Maya said, purposefully changing the subject.

"You can try. I don't know if anyone will listen, but you can try."

Maya leaned forward on the kitchen table and started rubbing her temples again. Who were you even supposed to tell about this sort of thing? She didn't know anyone in government and would have to figure out where to start. First, though, she needed to get out of the house. She rose from the table, patted her father awkwardly on the shoulder, and went down to the basement to haul up the bicycle she stored there.

Riding her bike made Maya feel young again, and before she knew it, she was at the library, a trip she'd taken a thousand times as a kid. She parked the bike in the rack out front and went in to start searching the card catalog for books about Sri Lanka and its history. She made a mental note to ask the reference librarian about how you were supposed to contact representatives, then went to the shelves and started pulling books.

After several hours of reading, Maya shifted in her chair and checked her watch. Everything she'd read had only confused her more. She thought that maybe if she talked about what she'd experienced, it would help organize her thoughts and take some of the power away from her nightmares. Talking to Kelsie was the obvious choice, and Maya wanted to see her, anyway. She also needed to get in touch with Sister Lucy, who had an uncanny ability to dole out just the right advice at the right time. Of course, there was always the risk that neither of them would care about what was happening in Sri Lanka, like the rest of the world, and Maya would have to be prepared for that, but reconnecting with these two people she loved couldn't hurt.

RADIO

Saturday morning, Maya's father was sitting on the bench near the front door pulling on his shoes.

"Are you going out? Where are you going?" Maya asked.

"Yes, I want to purchase a short-wave radio," her father said. "I'll be able to pick up the signal for the British news reports, and even reports from Asia."

"Oh, wow. You can get news from all over on one of those radios?"

Her father nodded. "And since Sri Lanka is still part of the British Commonwealth, maybe England will be reporting the news there."

"Ok, maybe I'll go with you. Let me just change my clothes."

Maya had never been to the store they went to, but her father seemed to know his way around. The man at the counter had gold rings on two of his knuckles, disheveled hair, and was wearing a plaid shirt about two sizes too small. Underneath the glass countertop he was leaning on was a wonderland of electronics and gadgets.

Her father haggled over the price of the three different short-wave radios he was considering. He peppered the man with questions. Were they reliable? How long had they been sitting in the shop? Where were they made? Were they originals or knockoffs? Finally he chose one and they settled on a price.

Maya and her father returned home with the new radio wrapped in cellophane. Maya watched with fascination as her father fiddled with it, tuning the radio with a delicate dance of very slight adjustments to the dial and bending the antennae in various directions to try to catch a signal. Her father found several stations of interest, and so for the next few hours they listened to radio reports, trying to discern fact from fiction about the various attacks and government and international responses. Maya stifled a yawn as her father said, for the hundredth time, that what is *not* said in the news is as important as what is said.

"So, it sounds like there's no economic reason for anyone to care about the humanitarian crisis in Sri Lanka, even though thousands may have been killed," Maya said. "It's not like there's oil there."

"No, but there are some very important products. Textiles, rubber, tea. Cinnamon and precious gems, too," her father said. "But Sri Lanka is not the most important source of these goods. And these things are much less important than avoiding a nuclear war between the US and the Soviet Union."

"So no one will care." Maya sighed.

"But the people there in my community have always been talented and have always tried to find a way to make it on their own. They studied under the British system, you know, and are very well-educated."

"But didn't everything change after the British left in 1948?" Maya asked.

He nodded. "People started coalescing in groups based on language or religion. The leaders of the majority, the Sinhalese, started talking about one language only, and favoring one religion only, Buddhism. They were angry that the British had not given them equal opportunities in the past," her father said.

"Then the people who weren't on the right side of language or religion or ethnicity were targeted?" Maya asked. When her father nodded, she said, "Is that the reason we left? Or because my mother was American?"

Maya's father ignored the question, as he usually did when she asked about her mother. Watching his face, Maya suddenly realized how painful the topic must be for her father. She'd never quite grasped that before, what life must have been like for her father after his wife died, and the lack of photos of her mother in the house suddenly made sense. Maya looked at her father and yearned for a simple hug, but that was something he was unaccustomed to because of the way he was raised.

"We left because I saw that the oppression would not stop," he said finally. "We left to seek opportunities elsewhere. My education gave us a chance to leave." He paused, then said, "We were lucky."

DREAMS

Maya's nightmares became more frequent, and she would wake many mornings on a tear-soaked pillowcase. She couldn't shake the violent images in her head of the men's throats being slit and the smell of the housekeeper's flesh, nor could she shake her memory of the philosophy professor's voice that she had heard in the stairwell as she and her father escaped the hospital. Though her father was skeptical that anything a doctor in America could do would help, he relented and accompanied Maya to consult with a physician when she told him she hadn't slept in weeks.

The physician took her blood pressure and then asked her to lie down on the black vinyl examination table. He looked into her eyes with a light, applied pressure to the sides of her throat and temples, then asked her a series of questions about her symptoms and anything unusual she had observed or experienced recently. After she answered, he turned to Maya's father.

"She seems stressed. It's a new concept in the medical community they're calling post-traumatic stress disorder. I can't be certain, because it could also just be a high amount of temporary stress."

The doctor seemed to remember Maya was in the room then and turned back to her. "That might be why you're having bad dreams. Can you tell me more about the dreams?"

"Post-traumatic stress disorder?" Maya asked, ignoring his question about the dreams.

"Yes. It's not uncommon after traumatic events to have continuing feelings of distress," the doctor explained. "Or even during unusually stressful transition periods."

Maya didn't respond, nor did her father. How do you talk about something so violent and terrible? How do you bring up ethnic cleansing in a medical appointment?

"Is there something unusual going on right now in your family's life? Something that might be unusually stressful?" the doctor asked. "You've just graduated college, right? Have you been treated before for anything like this? A trauma you experienced in the past?"

Maya's father seemed to be considering what to say.

"We have packed up and moved a few times now," he said finally. "We immigrated here and have moved within the US. And Maya is embarking on a new job search."

"I moved back home so I can find a job and apply to graduate school," Maya said.

"That could be it," the doctor said, turning away from Maya. "Transition."

Maya sat up. "Actually, there is something that is causing me stress. I just wasn't sure how to discuss it."

"What is it?" the physician asked, turning toward Maya again.

"We only just made it back to this country a few weeks ago," Maya said, unable to stop the words from escaping her lips. "We got caught in some violent riots in Asia. We were assaulted and chased by mobs who were trying to kill us, and who killed others in front of us. I don't even want to describe the horrific details to you. We barely escaped. We had to live in a makeshift refugee camp for several days without food or water or knowing whether we were ever going to leave that place alive."

The doctor stared at Maya awkwardly, his mouth gaping open.

DREAMS

Maya's father cut through the silence. "This has been most informative, doctor. We don't want to burden you with this information. Is there anything we can do about the stress?" he asked, as if it were his responsibility to placate the doctor.

The physician cleared his throat. "I'm sorry. I don't know what to say. It sounds terrible. I do recommend some sort of treatment."

The doctor said that medicine would only provide a temporary fix, and he recommended psychotherapy, talk therapy, with a specialist.

Maya had heard about talk therapy from her friends in college. She had also heard that it didn't always help, and could take months or even years to work if it did.

"Is there nothing that can help immediately?" Maya asked.

"I'm sorry," the physician said. "It can take a long time to unpack these symptoms and learn how to cope with something like this. What you have been through sounds…quite unusual and very serious."

"What about meditation?" Maya asked, thinking again about the philosophy professor she'd met through Sister Lucy years earlier, the man whose voice had come back to her with startling clarity in the stairwell. She had been pleasantly surprised to be introduced to another Asian person in the area, and Sister Lucy had spoken highly of him, vouching for him, and gushing about how much she respected him and his gentle nature. He'd tried to explain meditation to her, but had warned that there were things she needed to do before beginning to meditate.

"*When there is a mismatch between reality and expectations,*" he'd said, "*people feel disappointed, stressed, and frustrated. But the key is to take your energy away from negative things and move toward more positive things. Don't dwell on the past. Focus on changing yourself—your perspective, your reactions, your actions—first. Put realistic positive thoughts inside your head. Your life becomes what you think, Maya, so you must be careful with your thoughts because they become your behaviors and actions and consequences. Make this a deliberate effort, every day. Only when this becomes a habit can you use meditation to get to the next stage."*

"I've heard about meditation, but it's not widely used right now," the doctor said. "There is a lot more research to be done. Plus, I don't know if we fully understand the benefits, or how quickly it can improve a patient's condition."

Maya's shoulders slumped. There was so much to do between the job search and grad school applications, and she needed to be able to sleep through the night and concentrate during the day. She needed to move on.

DESIRE

Lying in her bed at night, unable to sleep yet again, Maya tried to recall anyone she'd ever known who had some sort of influence. After the appointment with the doctor, she'd realized that the only way for her to move on was to *do something* with what she'd been through in Sri Lanka, and that meant telling someone who might be able to use her story in a positive way. Sadly, as she flipped her pillow and tried to summon sleep, the name she kept coming back to was Jeev.

Through the hometown grapevine, she'd heard that her former nemesis was working at a lobbying firm in Washington, D.C., a job he'd gotten through his father's connections. The thought of re-connecting with Jeev made her head hurt, but Maya needed help, and she didn't know anyone else in Washington.

The next morning, she called 411 and got the number for his firm, then asked the receptionist who answered for Jeev's office. She was on hold for a few minutes before he picked up.

"Who is this?"

"It's Maya. Do you remember me?"

Silence.

"From Pennsylvania," Maya said.

More silence.

"From high school," Maya said.

"Oh… Maya. What do you want?"

"I need to speak to someone about getting in front of my Congressional representatives."

Jeev didn't respond.

"It's literally a matter of life and death. Not mine, but other people. In another country. They're at war."

"I see," Jeev said. "Why would you want to do that?"

"Something happened this past summer. Something I saw."

"What?"

"It was bad…gruesome, actually. And I know it's something the government, our government, will want to know. Maybe even your firm."

"You know, you spend too much time worrying about other people. I'm sure they're not thinking about you."

"Wait—what? So you would rather let people suffer?" Maya said, stunned by Jeev's response.

Jeev sighed audibly.

"Can we talk in person?" Maya said. "I don't know if this is something we should discuss over the telephone."

"I'm pretty busy."

"I understand," Maya said, forcing herself to sound warm and friendly. "I know we haven't spoken in years."

"And I don't recall parting on the best of terms."

"No, you're right," Maya said. "But this is not for me. This is to help people who are suffering through war, and what seems like ethnic cleansing."

Jeev sighed again. "Fine. When? Are you coming to Washington?"

"I…err…I don't even have a car right now. Are you ever back home?"

"I don't know, Maya. I might be, in a couple of weeks," Jeev said.

"Can we talk then?"

"Fine."

"Okay. Thanks. I'll speak to you then," Maya said.

"Yep. I'll try to remember to call you when I'm back," Jeev said, then hung up.

BICYCLE

The truth sat bare and ugly in front of Maya. She needed to navigate its sinewy path with care and conviction if anything she was going to do stood a chance of making a difference. At the same time, her feeling that things were not moving fast enough was acute and unrelenting, and she had convinced herself that she was at fault for some of that. She was feeling uncertain in her actions. Was she taking the right steps? She stared up at the ceiling from her bed, feeling unusually groggy.

The morning after her conversation with Jeev, Maya woke with a desperate need to reconnect with the only truly close friend she'd had growing up, Kelsie. Kelsie had moved home after college to commute to work in Pittsburgh while she was saving up money to get her own apartment. It made for a long workweek, so Maya hadn't wanted to bother her, but she really needed to confide in Kelsie and get her advice about how to process what had happened in Sri Lanka. Plus, Kelsie's father was an attorney and on the town council, and maybe he'd have some advice about who to contact.

As she cycled to Kelsie's house, Maya remembered her first dinner there, and how shocked she'd been to find that Kelsie's family ate together, and at a set time every night. Maya had never known a particular dinner time growing up. No one was ever waiting for her for dinner.

Maya shoved the kickstand down with her right foot and looked up at Kelsie's house, then at the neatly trimmed bushes that flanked the entryway, the freshly cut lawn, and the zinnias that lined the walkway. She approached Kelsie's front door and raised her hand to knock, but suddenly everything went black.

Maya awoke to Kelsie tapping her on the shoulder as she lay on the front steps.

"Kels. What happened?" Maya asked, blinking.

"I don't know. You were just lying here by the door when I opened it," Kelsie said.

"Oh."

"How long have you been here?"

"I don't know," Maya said.

"C'mon. Let me help you get up," Kelsie said, reaching for Maya.

As they walked inside, Maya looked at her friend. Even in gray sweatpants, with her strawberry blonde hair in a ponytail, freckle-cheeked Kelsie was lovely.

"What is going on, Maya?" Kelsie said. "You look exhausted. And stressed."

"Nothing. It's nothing. Tell me about you, Kels."

They sat down on the couch and Kelsie told Maya about her new job marketing for a foundation, and how things had been going for her during her transition back to their hometown.

"I don't know, Maya. This is an okay job for now. I just don't feel…" Kelsie's voice tapered off.

"What?"

"I just don't feel like I'm doing anything meaningful."

"That's okay, right? I think that's probably normal for a first job?"

"I guess so," Kelsie said, sweeping a few loose strands of hair into her ponytail. "And I thought I had met someone special a few months ago, but…that didn't pan out." Kelsie sighed.

"Oh, Kels," Maya said. "Do you want to talk about it?"

"Nah. I just need to move on. My dad says I should go to Norway and spend time with my grandparents, maybe explore some opportunities there, and see the world."

"That sounds pretty great."

"Maybe."

"So when did you get your ears triple pierced?" Maya said.

Kelsie instinctively reached for her ears. "Oh these," she said blushing. "I got it done recently. Mom and Dad weren't happy at first, but they realize I'm an adult now."

"Wow. I would have never been allowed more than one piercing," Maya said, "and you've got three in each ear!"

Kelsie smiled. "I was feeling wild, I guess. I needed to cheer myself up after we…after that guy and I didn't work out."

Maya wished she had had more of Kelsie's kind of spunk growing up. Maybe then she would be able to deal with what she'd experienced better.

Kelsie looked at Maya, who had begun rubbing her temples.

"Okay, Maya. Out with it. Don't pretend. I know something is wrong."

"You're right. I just don't know where to begin," Maya said.

"My goodness, Maya, what is it?"

Maya began to tell Kelsie an edited version of her trip back to Asia. She only mentioned the atrocities she had witnessed in Sri Lanka, and didn't share any of the details about being attacked herself or staying in the refugee camp.

"That sounds awful. You saw all that?"

"The situation is terrible for the people there. There's violence and corruption, and blatant discrimination."

"How blatant?" Kelsie asked.

"Well, the university has quotas to keep people out. *That* kind of blatant."

"And people know about it?"

Maya nodded.

"And it's violent there?"

Maya nodded again. "Everything seems divided by race and language. Tamil versus Sinhalese. Even religion…"

Maya explained about the decades of violence, and the way the attacks were targeted on the Tamils using voter lists, and how even though many people felt the government was participating, no one seemed to care. She explained how the president had made public statements about mistreating and even starving the minorities, and how still no one had done anything.

"I just feel like I need to tell someone," Maya said. "Someone important. It's the only way to help." She looked at Kelsie. "Maybe that seems crazy, but aren't we responsible for the things we witness? And I was kind of hoping your dad might know someone I could talk to."

"Oh, I see," Kelsie said, leaning back on the couch, pondering what Maya had said.

"People just don't understand how bad it is there."

"Is there more that you're not telling me? I know you, and I feel that you're not telling me everything," Kelsie said, waiting for Maya to respond. When Maya shook her head, Kelsie said, "I'm sure it's been terrible for you."

"Thanks, Kels."

"Just tell me this. Forget about all the stuff in Sri Lanka. Are *you* ok? I mean, you passed out on my front lawn, Maya! Imagine if you went to open the door and I was lying on your front steps!" Kelsie smiled to take the sting out of her words, then placed her hand on Maya's arm. "I'm just worried about you, that's all."

"I've been having bad dreams that keep me up at night, and I think I'm just exhausted. I even went to see a doctor. He thought I was stressed, but he didn't really understand…"

Kelsie reached for Maya and wrapped her in a hug. "Well,

you fainted on my porch," she said when she let go. "So maybe he's right?"

"Maybe."

"You've got to take care of yourself, Maya. Don't take on too much."

"That's funny. My father said the same thing."

"Maybe he's right, too. Don't ignore your health."

They sat in silence for a few minutes, then Kelsie said, "You know what? Maybe my dad does know someone. I mean he's just in local politics, but maybe." She turned toward Maya on the couch. "But in the meantime, I know what you should do. You should talk to Jase."

Maya crinkled her forehead in confusion.

"Remember Jase? The debate guy in school?"

"Oh, right. But why talk to him?"

"Well, he might be able to give you some tips. And he's home right now. I saw him the other day in town."

"I kind of lost touch with him after high school," Maya said, rubbing her temples again. A headache was coming on fast. "I better get going," she said, getting up from the couch. "My head is really starting to hurt."

Kelsie gave Maya another hug and walked her out.

As much as Maya's head was pounding on the ride home, she felt better after talking to Kelsie. It was good to have an ally.

COOTIES

Maya was sweating from pedaling uphill as she returned home, but the exercise seemed to have knocked her headache back a bit. After the conversation with Kelsie, she was focused on telephoning Jase right away. She parked her bicycle near the front door, ran into the house, and reached for the telephone. But when it was in her hand, she hesitated. What would Jase think after not hearing from her for all these years? He had witnessed several of her most humiliating moments in high school—moments that left an indelible mark in her own memory—and Maya wondered if he would even want to speak to her.

She looked up his number in the phone book and dialed. No answer. She checked the number and dialed again, but there was still no answer, and there did not seem to be an answering machine.

"Maya, who are you calling?" her father asked, entering the kitchen.

"What are you doing at home, Dad?" Maya asked, hanging up the telephone.

"It's the weekend, remember?"

"Oh, right."

"What's going on?" her father said, placing his hands on his hips. "You look lost in thought."

"I just returned from Kelsie's house. Remember her?"

"Kelsie. Yes, of course."

"She suggested I reach out to our old classmate, Jase."

"Jase? Is that a male name? I don't remember him. Why would you call this boy?" her father asked, instantly suspicious.

"She said he might be able to help me with a project I'm working on."

"I see," Maya's father said. "A project."

Maya realized her father was worried about old traditions, about the image of engaging in inappropriate behaviors before marriage, so she tried to divert the conversation.

"I'm slightly mortified to reach out, though," she said, sliding into a chair at the kitchen table.

"Why is that?"

"Oh, several embarrassing incidents, back in our school days."

"Like what?"

"Well, on my first day of sophomore year, right after we moved here, I was so nervous I felt sick all day at school. I thought I was going to be teased about my clothes again."

"Why teased? I always thought you looked very nice."

"Dad, c'mon! I wore bell-bottom plaid pants and shirts that didn't match!"

"So? That was still in style back then, no?"

"Bell-bottoms, yeah. But plaid ones?" Maya shook her head. "And especially not with odd shirts that didn't match. Anyway, that first day, I was grouped with Kelsie and Jase in my classes."

"I don't really remember that boy. You never spoke of him."

"He was very smart. In the gifted program at school. But he ended up in classes with me and Kelsie because some of the classes were mixed levels."

"I never knew that."

"I think his whole family was gifted. Both of his parents were teachers and members of something called the Lions Club."

Maya paused, thinking back to the stories she had heard about Jase. "Jase was also mechanically gifted. He could build things, and he did special weekend programs with his mother or father or the Boy Scouts. He did wilderness excursions, and went on bike rides and camping trips, and helped out with the pinewood derby, too."

"Pinewood derby?" Maya's father asked. "What's that?"

"Younger scouts build wooden cars to race. And then have a big party for the winners with spaghetti and meatballs."

"That all sounds very admirable, I guess," Maya's father said.

"So you can see how I would feel inadequate around Jase at school? Keep in mind, I was the new kid and I looked different, plus I had those clothes."

"And this is how you judged yourself? On clothes?"

"It's America, Dad. And we do look different," Maya said. "I still look different." She sighed. "People were not used to us. There was a whole group of kids who told me I had cooties on the first day of school, in front of everyone."

"What is cooties?"

"I had no idea! But it turns out it's a childhood thing, something little kids say to tease others. It means you have lice."

"Why would high school students say this?"

"I don't know, Dad. But I knew it was bad and I was so embarrassed. And that was my first day in that school. And it didn't get much better."

"What else happened?" Maya's father asked.

"I was in the science lab with Kelsie and Jase, and we were supposed to be dissecting a frog. And guess who was the science teacher? Mrs. H., our neighbor."

"Mrs. H? The lady from down the street?"

"Here, hold this," Jase had said, pulling one of the frog's legs. "We need to pin this one."

"Is it okay to touch it directly?" Maya asked.

"Sure. It's preserved with formaldehyde."

Maya picked up the scalpel lying on the dissection board. "I can do the cutting."

"Do you know where to cut?" Kelsie asked.

Mrs. H. was walking around the room, checking on the dissection groups, and as she got to Maya's group, she stopped.

"Do you know what you are doing, Maya?" she said, her hands on her wide hips. "Do you even understand English?"

Maya nodded silently and wished the ground would open up and swallow her.

"We'll see," Mrs. H. said, and moved on to the next group.

Jase helped Maya pin the legs as Kelsie went to wash her hands at the sink in the corner. Maya prepared to start cutting. Her hair, which Maya's father cut for her, was pulled back in a short ponytail for the class, but a piece was too short for the ponytail and kept swinging into Maya's cheek and eye. She didn't want to touch her hair or face with frog-tainted fingers, so she blew out of the side of her mouth to move the hair. It moved, but came right back, so she blew again.

"Here, let me do it," Jase said.

"No, I'm ok," Maya said.

But Jase reached out, anyway, swiping the piece of hair off her face and tucking it behind Maya's ear for her. His hand felt cold and Maya jerked her head back in surprise.

"Sorry. I thought that would help," Jase said.

This got Maya thinking about the comment in the hallway earlier.

"Hey," she asked Jase as Kelsie rejoined them. "What are cooties?"

"Cooties are lice," Jase replied. "It's something kindergarteners say."

"Lice! I...but I don't have lice," Maya said. "Why would someone say that?"

"Oh, those students are silly, Maya. Don't pay attention to them. They say that to...to...people who look different," Kelsie said.

It was a trait Maya would grow to really value, Kelsie's tactful way of combining kindness and empathy with the truth.

"And we don't get many around here," Jase added. "People who are different, I mean."

Maya had noticed. She was about to respond when the school principal called her into the hallway to ask her loudly what all the talk about cooties was and did she need to see the school nurse?

Maya was mortified and tried to think quickly on her feet.

"My father gave me medicine for my hair," she lied. "It's gone."

The principal looked at Maya through her thick, square-framed glasses for a moment, then tilted her head and looked to the side, cupping her chin in one hand. Finally, she looked back at Maya and said, "Okay, I see. Thank you."

Maya watched the principal walk down the hallway, her thick body encased in a mint green skirt suit and beige low heels. As she walked back into the classroom, both Kelsie and Jase locked eyes with Maya.

"Oh Maya..." Kelsie said sympathetically.

"You never told me about that all these years," Maya's father said softly when she finished recounting the story. "And I don't know why you would pay attention to mindless teasing." Maya's father shook his head. "But it sounds like Kelsie and Jase were very kind."

"I suppose you're right. And maybe I didn't tell you because I was always nervous about getting good grades and never wanted you to think there was trouble at school."

Maya sat at the kitchen table while her father grabbed a glass of water and left without responding. She rose from her chair and tried dialing Jase's parents' home one more time, but again there was no response on the other end, and no answering machine so she could leave a message.

Never mind, Maya thought, and rummaged through the kitchen drawers for the paper her father kept there. She pulled out a nice piece of note paper and started composing a letter to her government representatives in Congress.

She wrote what she knew, incorporating some of her research from the library. She tried to be factual but also appeal to their sense of humanity.

She was almost through when her father returned to the kitchen, visibly agitated.

"What's wrong?"

"I just read a letter from relatives in Sri Lanka," her father replied.

"And what happened? You seem irritated."

"One of my distant cousins reports that a school in a village near their town has an infestation of lice. They had never even heard of lice before in this village," her father exclaimed.

"That's ironic," Maya said.

It was hard to muster up the enthusiasm for her father's attachment to the unimportant minutiae in Sri Lanka. She understood on some level, but she also yearned for him to balance his intense interest in his homeland with more effort to integrate here. She had never really heard him talk much about what he did at work or his colleagues there. They'd been in the US for several years now, and he still was not fully assimilated. And what was worse, he didn't even seem to notice that he wasn't assimilated. Somehow, that kept Maya from feeling fully assimilated, too.

The truth was that after a decade in America, Maya did not

feel fully accepted in either the US *or* in Sri Lanka. Part of it was because they'd had to leave almost all of their personal belongings behind when they immigrated to the States, and then had rented a furnished apartment, so she'd always lived among someone else's stuff, wearing someone else's clothing. Even now, in this home an hour from Pittsburgh where they'd moved just before Maya's sophomore year of high school, there was an air of temporariness and transition. Kelsie's home was full of family photographs and belongings with memories attached, but Maya often felt that she and her father and the twins could be replaced by another family without much effort. Who would know they'd been there at all? And with her father's thoughts and attention so firmly planted back in Sri Lanka, Maya yearned to finally feel fully present in one place.

HOTLINE

One of the many things Kelsie and Maya had bonded over was their affection for Sister Lucy. They both admired and understood her. Sister Lucy was positive and joyful, and Maya and Kelsie both appreciated that she was one of the only adults in their microcosm who did not seem judgmental. She was unconditionally caring and dedicated to her students, and her calmness and tolerance pervaded the classroom. She was exactly what young adults needed, and became like family to Maya, Kelsie, and many other students.

After speaking with Kelsie, Maya was even more convinced that talking to Sister Lucy about what had happened to her was a good idea. Sister Lucy would have objective, thoughtful advice. So Maya went to the peer counseling and crisis hotline center near the Catholic church in the center of town where she knew Sister Lucy would be working now that she had retired from teaching. She walked up the front stairs and knocked on the door.

When the door opened, Maya was greeted by a familiar face. Sister Lucy had always reminded her a bit of her grandmother Esther, her father's mother.

"Maya! How wonderful to see you! But what are you doing here?" Sister Lucy exclaimed.

"How are you, Sister? I haven't seen you in a while."

"Good, good," Sister Lucy said, grabbing Maya's arm and pulling her inside the door. "Come, Maya. Come in."

"Thank you," Maya said, stepping inside.

She was not surprised to see that the room was still drab, brown, and depressing. It had always smelled musty, too, and the furniture was donated and outdated, with a table at one corner with a blue rotary phone and a lamp on it, and an orange cushioned chair with rectangular pillows. There was a window above the table, with old aluminum blinds that were partially open to allow slivers of sunlight to pass through, and the walls were concrete brick, painted in a dark cream color. The peer counseling group never had enough funds to renovate, or graduate to a better space. Just enough to pay a small rent for this space and the phone bills, and to fund a minimal amount of training and publicity.

Maya looked at Sister Lucy, who wasn't wearing her nun's habit. Instead, she had on a short-sleeved button-down shirt, untucked, that seemed to be the wrong size for her stomach and large chest, and a khaki skirt and brown sandals, the kind families who hiked wore. Her hair was shorter now, brownish, and feathered back on both sides. She was plumper, and her cheeks were rosy, as was her nose.

"What brings you here?" Sister Lucy asked.

"I'm back from college, staying at my father's home while I do my job search and apply to graduate school."

"Oh, that's nice. And you came to see me?" Sister Lucy asked, clearly surprised.

In that moment, Maya realized that Sister Lucy had never known how important she was to her, to Kelsie, and to a number of other students. She had never really understood that she was salvation for teenagers desperate to be understood and accepted. She probably also had never fully grasped the positive impact of her jovial personality, her respect for the students, her tolerance of their antics. Maya felt a pang of sadness that Sister Lucy had probably never realized she was an inspiration to so many students.

"Yes, Sister. I came to see you."

"Whatever for, Maya? Although I'm delighted that you did."

Maya cleared her throat and hesitated.

"What is it, dear?"

Maya looked up and met Sister Lucy's kind eyes. "There's something I need to share with you. I don't know what to do."

"Oh, dear. Then first, sit down."

Maya took a seat on the orange cushioned chair and put her hands in her lap. She shuffled her feet.

"I saw something, Sister. Something terrible," Maya began. "And I don't know what to do about it."

"Yes?"

"This past summer." Maya paused. She didn't think she needed to share every last gory detail with Sister Lucy, just enough to make an impact. "I was visiting my birth country, Sri Lanka."

"Go on," Sister Lucy prompted.

"I was attacked by people in the streets. By a mob. Me and my father. Along with thousands of other people who were attacked, too, in their homes, shops, streets, and the train stations. It went on for days."

Sister Lucy reeled back on her chair. "What? Attacked how?"

"They were trying to kill us. One man was going to try to rape me, but my father was able to pull me free. We ran for our lives."

"My goodness, dear." Sister Lucy grabbed Maya's hands. "How did you escape? Are you okay now?"

"My father and I made it to a refugee camp. We were there for several days, and then we finally were able to get back to my grandmother's house and get my brothers. I went on the first bus and then my father came, but while we were there…" Maya stopped herself, realizing that she was on the verge of saying too much. "I'll spare you all the disturbing details, but I will tell you that I witnessed things that no human should have to witness."

"You and your father must have had a terrible time of it. Were your brothers involved, too?"

"No, no. Thank goodness. No. The twins were spared. They weren't with us," Maya said.

"That must have been very difficult," Sister Lucy said, releasing Maya's hands and making the sign of the cross on her forehead and chest. "Are you sure you are okay?" she asked.

"I think so. But I don't know what to do with what I saw. I feel like I need to tell people who can help, organizations who can help, about what's going on there."

"To help you, or—?"

Maya shook her head. "To help the whole country. Thousands of people have already died. Tens of thousands are homeless now. People are trying to flee the country, but it's so difficult."

"Thousands? Maya, please forgive my ignorance, but I don't know much about Sri Lanka. What's the root of all this violence?"

"There's a long history there of violence against ethnic minorities. Well, violence and oppression. My mother was American, mixed I've been told, and my father is mixed, too, because his mother is British. But the other half of us is Tamil, which is an ethnic minority there. And there are systems in place that make it hard for minorities to succeed. My father was an excellent student, but he was denied a place at university because he is Tamil. That's what I mean."

Sister Lucy nodded.

"We were able to come to the US because of my father's work, and also because my mom was American, I guess, although she was already gone. So we're lucky. We don't have to live in all that violence."

"The things humans do to one another…" Sister Lucy said, then let her voice trail off.

"The people who are still stuck there need help, though. Not everyone can get out, even if a country would take them in as refugees," Maya said, "even though war has broken out."

Sister Lucy nodded. "Yes, I remember the efforts to bring people from Vietnam and Cambodia. Church groups all over the country sponsored people to come here, but still, it wasn't an easy process."

Maya nodded. "That's what needs to happen now. Do you know anyone, or any organizations, that could help?"

Maya waited as Sister Lucy thought for several minutes.

"There are a few organizations I know of, linked to the Church," she said finally. "They have a solid track record of helping in these types of situations."

"That's why I came to see you, Sister. You always said that doing for others is the best way to heal ourselves. I feel like if I do something for the people left over there, then maybe I can help myself, too," Maya said. "Can you contact the church organizations?"

"Keep in mind, Maya, that I'm just one little nun. Oftentimes the most I can do is pray."

"Yes, please pray. But I do think your calls would make a difference."

Sister Lucy didn't respond, and Maya wondered if there was a reason she was reluctant to act, or if she simply felt powerless to do much for a situation so far removed from Pennsylvania.

"Or, you could give me the contact information and introductions, and I can contact them instead?" Maya asked.

"Yes, of course. We can contact them," Sister Lucy said.

"There must also be various Catholic dioceses in northern and southern Sri Lanka, right?" Maya suggested.

"I don't know, dear. I'll look into that."

"There must be, Sister. I remember my grandmother knowing

of Catholics around Sri Lanka. Can we contact them, also, the dioceses? Tell them what I know and what I saw?"

"Yes, that's a good idea. I don't know why I didn't think of that," Sister Lucy said, sounding flustered.

"Maybe someone at one of these organizations is already in touch with someone in the diocese there. Surely they're aware of what's going on?"

"Perhaps."

"What about the International Red Cross? Should we contact them? Check if there is anyone on the ground there? Or whether they plan to send people?"

"I don't know enough yet, Maya. I'll have to find out in the next few days."

"Thank you, Sister," Maya said.

Sister Lucy grabbed Maya's hands again, as if to reassure her. "I will find out how to contact these organizations. I will talk to the priest here about talking to the Bishop. I will see what I can do to help you."

She squeezed Maya's hands, then let go and sat back in her chair. She seemed to be lost in thought.

"What is it, Sister?" Maya asked.

"I'm thinking about what you went through, Maya, and how to help you. I don't want to lose sight of your needs in our efforts to help other people," Sister Lucy said. "I've just realized that there may be someone who would be a wonderful resource for you. Someone who will understand."

"What kind of person? A priest?"

Sister Lucy shook her head. "No, not exactly. But first, I have the numbers of a few therapists and I want you to consider talking to someone. You've been through something very shocking, and you need to process those emotions, not bury them."

Maya looked down and nodded. "I haven't really talked to

anyone about my personal experience since I got back, and I know I need to… I've been having bad dreams and waking up sad some mornings."

"I'll give you two numbers before you leave," Sister Lucy said. "And there is someone else, too, as I said before. It's a bit of a long shot, but maybe there is something he can do, though I'm not yet sure what or how."

Maya raised her eyebrows in question.

"Do you remember the man I introduced you to years ago, the former monk who became a philosophy professor?"

Maya had remembered the philosophy professor well even before his voice had come back to her with such force during the tense moment in the stairwell in Sri Lanka. He had made a huge impact on Maya. They'd even spoken on the telephone a few times after they'd met years ago at the crisis center with Sister Lucy, because the professor had recommended a book and asked Maya to let him know what she thought. So she'd called him at his office to discuss it two or three times. She had thought of him on several occasions more recently, too, but somehow she had forgotten completely that he used to be a monk.

"I do remember him, yes, of course, but, uhh… I'm not sure about meeting with him." The thought of being alone now in close quarters with any man made Maya's skin crawl, even a man Sister Lucy thought so highly of and she already somewhat knew.

Sister Lucy inspected Maya's face, then nodded. "I understand. I'm sure he'd be willing to talk on the phone. Or perhaps it's not the right idea."

"Oh, no. He has been so helpful to me in the past and is so full of wisdom. I really would like to speak to him again. I don't think I could grasp everything he said before. Maybe I was too young… Or maybe I just never made enough of an effort."

Even though they'd only spoken a few times, when Maya had recognized the voice in the stairwell as the professor's, it hadn't entirely surprised her. He'd always struck Maya as someone she should feel fortunate to know, someone who, like Sister Lucy, was going to have an outsized influence on her.

"Tell me again, Sister, how do you know him? I've forgotten," Maya said.

"We met through an interfaith food pantry that supports the surrounding towns," Sister Lucy explained. "That was before he began teaching at Duquesne."

"That's one of the places I am applying to graduate school."

"Oh! Wonderful. Well, perhaps you can visit him on campus," she said. "But, you know, I believe he actually lives around here, near Somerset somewhere."

Maya looked up. "Does he? I haven't spoken to him in a while."

"Reach out to him again," Sister Lucy said. "He might be helpful."

"You said he was a former monk, though? A Buddhist monk?" Maya asked. "I didn't know that."

"Yes, and I've always found him to be unusually wise in the matters of life," Sister Lucy said. "But Maya, you shouldn't take on all of this on your own. It's too much."

"Sri Lanka is a Buddhist country," Maya said. "But Buddhism has been politicized, and even driven people to violence at times."

"What do you mean?" Sister Lucy asked. "I've always believed Buddhists are generally against violence."

Maya nodded. "They are. But back in the 1950s, the politicians in Sri Lanka campaigned on the idea of one language and favoring one religion—Buddhism—treating all other languages and religions as inferior. They implemented single language requirements, which made it difficult for minorities to access jobs, and people protested."

"I can imagine," Sister Lucy said, nodding.

"The Buddhist monks counter-protested," Maya said. "It led to riots and killing, and then the quotas for university I told you about. There were more riots and killings in the 1970s, and even today, some Buddhist monks are advocating for the oppression of religious minorities and even instigating violence at times."

"I don't know what to say, Maya. That's so disappointing."

"Some of the riots this past summer were led by Buddhist monks."

Sister Lucy nodded. "Well, I know this man, Maya. He is a good man who would not support such things."

"No, I know. You've always spoken highly of him."

"My immediate concern is for you. You've been through something horrible and you need to talk to someone, and I think he'd be a wonderful resource."

Maya thought for a moment, then said, "Ok. Maybe I'll try to speak to him again."

#

Maya's father was at the kitchen table when she got home from visiting Sister Lucy.

"Hi," he said, looking up from his papers. "Where were you?"

"I was visiting Sister Lucy at the crisis hotline."

"A hotline? Hotline for what purpose?"

"It is for peer counseling, for people in moments of crisis. I used to volunteer there before college, remember?"

Maya's father shook his head. "No, I don't remember that. But why did you go there? Is something wrong?"

"No, no. I was just visiting Sister Lucy. Being there did bring back a lot of memories, though. Conversations I had when I was answering the hotline."

As soon as she'd walked into the crisis center, Maya had felt odd, as if something repressed was trying to bubble to the surface inside her.

Her father examined Maya's face. "I think these hotlines are useful. When I was growing up, our neighbor's son became very desperate. He could have used that kind of help."

"What did he do?"

"I think for some reason he didn't get along with people in his home. He lived with his mother and grandfather. His father had died in a car accident."

"So he was sad about that?"

"I imagine so. But he was targeted, picked on in town, because he was a Tamil minority, and a Christian on top of that. And sometimes he quarreled with people and caused trouble in town."

"Like what kind of trouble?"

"When other kids picked on him, he would fight back. And he used to quarrel with his mother and grandfather all the time. Sometimes we could hear them in the streets."

"So what happened to him?"

"One day he ingested kerosene. The kind used in lamps."

"That's so sad. How old was he?"

"Very young. Maybe a teenager."

Maya sat down in the chair across from her father. It was so tragic to hear that someone could have been so desperate at such a young age, but having worked at the crisis hotline and now having been through something that had left her feeling utterly powerless, she understood.

GLASSES

Maya was lost in thought in the stretching class when the young man on the mat in front of her initiated a friendly conversation. She had returned to her local gym to attend some exercise classes, hoping it would help her de-stress and feel calmer. Between college graduation and job searches and graduate school applications and her conviction to bring attention to what was going on in Sri Lanka, Maya felt like she'd been forced into adulthood far more abruptly than she would have liked. The stress of it all was wearing her down and she longed for someone to talk to who would help her make sense of everything and figure out a plan to move forward. She was really hoping that one of the people she'd reached out to—Sister Lucy or her Congressional representatives or even Jeev—would respond with ideas.

Maya had glanced at the young man when he first walked into the room at the beginning of class and had felt a tug of familiarity. He was unusually striking, with blondish-brownish hair and a sharp nose, but she could not immediately place him, and the instructor had started the class moments later and she'd had to focus. Now, as the instructor gave final tips on stretches that could be done at home, he turned to her.

"It's unbelievable how hard some of those stretches were," he said, swiveling on his mat to look at her.

Maya looked down. He was so handsome it made her stomach flutter. In school, no guy had ever really noticed Maya, at least not in the way she had wanted to be noticed. She'd chalked that up to having been the only girl in the classroom who looked different. Her golden skin tone and dark hair made her stand out, but not in the way she wanted.

"I know what you mean," Maya forced herself to say as she stretched her legs out in front of her and leaned back on both of her hands, suddenly aware of her loose jogging pants and plain t-shirt and short haircut and bare face.

"It's me, Jase, by the way. Do you remember me?" the young man said, extending his hand to Maya.

Maya's mouth fell open. "Jase? Is that really you?"

No wonder he looked familiar! It had been more than four years since they had last spoken or seen each other in person, but as Jase smiled, memories came flooding back.

Students were milling about on the asphalt by the school door, waiting their turn to walk back inside. Maya came up behind her classmate Janie, who was speaking with Jeev and some other girls. Janie was tall and preppy in her pink oxford and blue jeans. She had red hair, a large nose, crooked teeth and glasses, and was laughing her deep, guttural laugh. Suddenly she wheeled around and asked Maya why she was standing there, as if Maya was eavesdropping instead of simply standing in a crowd. Maya was taken by surprise and couldn't think of a response.

Janie repeated herself, her arms crossed, her mouth pouting. "I said, why are you standing there?"

She looked Maya up and down. Maya felt naked in her worn-out, hand-me-down dress.

"Where are you from, anyway?" Janie asked.

Maya didn't answer.

"Are you Spanish? Portuguese? Do you even speak English? And what is that dark spot on your arm?" Janie didn't wait for answers to any of her rapid-fire questions.

GLASSES

Maya looked down at her arm, at the smallpox vaccination scar that was a permanent reminder she'd been born in a place that needed a smallpox vaccination to travel and enter another country.

Jeev had been standing by Janie the whole time, whispering loudly in her ear. "Forget it, Janie. She's not worth your time" he sneered.

Jase, who had been watching from the line, spoke up. "Hey, why don't you leave her alone? She didn't do anything to anyone."

Maya turned to see who had spoken, who had defended her. The line was crowded and students were jostling each other in the commotion. Then Janie turned around, too, apparently done interrogating Maya, and as she did, her glasses fell off and landed on the asphalt. Jeev's foot grazed them just before Janie bent down to pick them up.

"My glasses!" Janie cried out.

"Look what you did," Jeev said to Maya as Janie inspected her now bent frames. Jeev stared at Maya for a few seconds, his ego so big it wore its own pair of trousers, then turned away and walked into the school building.

"Look what you did," Janie hissed at Maya before turning to follow Jeev inside.

"Hey guys, Maya didn't do anything. You know that," Jase called after them.

Maya was surprised to hear anyone defending her, especially Jase. It's not like they were friends. In fact, they hardly knew each other outside of class. But she didn't have much time to think about it because Mrs. H., her horrible neighbor and science teacher, yelled at the students to quiet down and get inside.

Maya headed toward her next class, which, unfortunately, was with all of them—Mrs. H., Janie, and Jeev. Mrs. H. told them to head into a small, dark room to watch a science film. One by one, the students took their seats in the makeshift media room. There was some commotion in the back while everyone waited for the film to start. Maya turned around to see what was going on. Janie was complaining to Mrs. H. about her glasses and Jeev was staring straight at Maya with the cruel snarl of a rabid dog.

Mrs. H. was glaring at Maya, too, and then she came forward to where Maya was sitting and asked Maya to follow her to the side of the room. Maya got up, confused.

"Did you do this?" Mrs. H. asked, holding up the slightly bent red glasses.

Maya was dumbfounded. "I…" Maya began. But she couldn't think of what to say that would both proclaim her innocence and keep her from tattling on Jeev.

"Well? I'm waiting."

When Maya didn't respond, Mrs. H. took her silence as an admission of guilt. She told Maya to sit on the side of the room away from the other students, where she would watch the movie alone.

Maya snapped out of her reverie and leaned forward towards Jase, her hand on the side of her face.

"Oh my goodness. I didn't recognize you at all! It's been years," Maya said.

"I'm sorry. I know we lost touch," Jase said.

"You look…so different."

"Yeah, well, I guess I grew, and lost some weight. My dad says I bloomed in college."

"What are you doing here?"

"I'm visiting my parents, but I just live in Pittsburgh. That's where I work. What are you doing here? Do you live here now?"

The flutters she felt were a strange new experience for Maya. She couldn't believe that Jase was bothering to talk to her when there were so many beautiful girls in the room. She forced herself to ignore the beating sensation in her abdomen and answer him.

"I'm just back here temporarily. I'm not sure for how long."

"In that case, do you want to take a walk with me? We could visit our old school grounds next door?"

"Huh? Oh, sure, but I'll need to grab my sweatshirt from the locker room," Maya said looking down at her exposed arms.

"I've got to grab my things, too. Shall we meet back in the lobby in a few minutes then?"

Maya nodded and headed to the women's locker room. She found it difficult to concentrate. Just a few weeks earlier she had only thought about reaching out to her old classmate for some pointers on writing a persuasive letter to her Congressman, maybe even public speaking, but now… Her stomach was doing flips at the thought of going for a simple walk with her old classmate.

As Maya reached the locker room and opened its door, she was relieved to find the space by her locker empty. She tried to imagine what she would say to Jase during their walk as she slipped her light blue sweatshirt over her head and headed back toward the gym lobby.

"Hey there, Maya! How are you?" It was a girl she recognized from high school, Pearl. Apparently, the gym was a hangout for her former classmates.

"Oh hi, Pearl. I'm sorry, I can't chat now. I'm headed out. Can we catch up later?" Maya asked, not waiting for Pearl's answer as she kept walking toward the lobby.

Pearl had been the type of girl who had really had it all together back in high school. She was half-Chinese and half-American, very well-dressed, organized, and a great soccer player. She had a boyfriend she'd met at a sports camp and even introduced to her parents. When Pearl told Maya that, sitting on the bleachers in the gym one day, Maya had felt a pang of envy. She could never even speak to her father about males. That was customary in Sri Lanka. She couldn't date until college, and even then, she wouldn't dare speak to her father about it. Sometimes Maya wondered how different her life might have been if her mother had lived. Her mother would have known how to navigate American culture, and how to navigate conversations with her father. But Maya was clueless, and as a result, never discussed boys at all, not even with Kelsie.

Jase was waiting for her in the lobby. She had not really noticed him, physically, back in high school when they were lab partners and teammates on the forensics club, but now she took a good look at him as she approached. He was several inches taller than her and had definitely become more attractive during college.

"It's really nice out today, better than what I would have expected for late Fall," Jase said as they started walking.

"Yes."

"Have you ever walked by the swimming pool? There's a nice path down there."

"Only a few times. I don't actually swim well, but I walked by a few times to see students practicing back when we were in school."

"Well, c'mon then," Jase said, holding out his elbow, waiting for Maya to lock her arm around it.

Maya was startled at first. She hadn't expected that, but she felt a warm sensation rippling throughout her body as she linked her arm through his. Jase's arm was firm, confident, self-assured, and warm. When he took her arm, it was as if he knew exactly what he was doing, exactly where he wanted to guide her. She enjoyed this feeling of being cared for, but she also couldn't look him in the eye. The nearness to him made her feel shy and self-conscious, especially because she suspected he was just being nice. There hadn't been very many non-American boys at any of the schools Maya had attended, and as she'd grown older, she'd realized that American boys didn't seem to want to date her. She didn't know why. Was it her skin color? Her exotic features?

"Maybe I could teach you to swim sometime?" Jase suggested, breaking the momentary silence.

"Uh huh," Maya replied, distracted by the nearness to him. They walked around the pool and the athletic fields and facilities, which were far enough away from the main building of the high school to guarantee a nice, long walk.

"Hey, Jase…"

"Yes?"

"I have to admit, this feels a bit strange. We weren't really that great of friends in high school. I mean, we were friends, but I guess I didn't really know you that well."

Jase opened his mouth as if to say something. Then he closed it and looked down. They walked for a few moments until he spoke.

"I guess you never knew that I liked you in high school, huh?"

"You did?" Maya said, then realized how shocked she sounded. "Really?"

"Yes."

"Why didn't you ever say anything?"

"I don't know." Jase paused. "We didn't see each other that often. We were only lab partners a few times. I only saw you occasionally during forensics club meetings. I figured you just never noticed me."

"Noticed you? Jase, I didn't think anybody ever noticed *me* back then."

"But I noticed you. I always noticed you."

"Then why didn't you talk to me more?"

Jase shrugged his shoulders. "I guess I was shy."

They both laughed lightly. How strange to think that Jase had liked her and been too shy to say it.

Maya wanted to revel in that moment, savor it, enjoy it. This was a milestone for her. However, she was starting to feel tense again and wasn't sure how to break the awkward moment.

"So, Jase…" she said.

"Yes?"

"Did you know that I tried to call you?"

"You did? When? Why?"

"A few weeks ago, but there was nowhere to leave a message."

"Why were you trying to reach me? I mean, I'm glad you tried to call. I'm just surprised."

Maya wasn't sure how comfortable she was sharing details with Jase, not right now, not at this stage when it felt like something might blossom between them. So she began slowly.

"I had a strange experience this past summer. I witnessed some terrible things."

"That sounds ominous. What kind of terrible things? Can you tell me about it?"

"I'm not sure if I feel comfortable sharing all the details yet…" Maya started. "But I think I need to get in front of someone in the government. Share what I witnessed."

Jase stopped walking and turned to stare at Maya. He let go of her arm. "The US government? Wow. It's that serious?"

Maya inspected Jase's face for signs of insincerity but found none.

"I think so… I mean, I wrote some letters, but it's not going to be enough. I need to do more, maybe request a meeting, maybe even try to approach someone in D.C. in person."

"Is that why you tried to call me? Because you wanted to talk about what to do?"

Maya nodded. "I was talking to Kelsie. Remember her?"

Maya waited for Jase to nod in acknowledgment before continuing.

"When I spoke with her, we realized we could use your help. Actually, Kelsie suggested it."

"Me?" Jase asked.

Maya nodded. "You know me. I never was that great at persuasive writing or public speaking. But now I see how it matters, how important it will be to what I'm trying to do. I am hoping to get an opportunity to tell people what I witnessed this past summer."

"Do you want—maybe if you told me what that was, I could help more?"

Maya hesitated. "I…I'm not sure if I've processed it all myself, actually."

Jase stared intently at Maya's face, examining it, as if he were trying to decode it. Then his expression softened.

"Okay, I can respect that. You know I'm happy to listen though, right? You can tell me whenever you're ready."

"Well, I thought trying to call you was a good idea. Remember how you helped me and Kelsie all those years ago? Remember how the school told us that we would be coached for the forensics team, and you stepped in when that coaching never materialized?"

"Vaguely," Jase responded, starting to walk again. "Sure, I think I remember now."

"It was when we hadn't done well in our first two competitions. Then you stepped in to help us prepare for our third. You helped us get better at getting our points across, and being more persuasive… You even coached us on how to deal with cheaters!" Maya said, falling into step with Jase.

"It's starting to come back to me."

"Do you remember what you said to us back then?"

"Not fully."

Maya looked up at him and paused for a moment, trying to recollect Jase's exact words back then.

"I never really forgot. It was great advice for the competition, but it was also great advice in general, for life."

"What did I say?"

"You said, 'It's probably too late to do anything about the cheaters in the past, but you can focus on improving and keep moving forward with your own standards, so that cheating won't matter.'"

#

Later that evening, still glowing from the walk with Jase, Maya passed by the kitchen and heard her father, who was reading the paper, mutter, "Nothing."

"What?" Maya asked, walking back to the kitchen.

"Nothing. There's absolutely nothing in the papers about the situation there."

"Where?" Maya asked, still lost in her own thoughts. She quickly registered what her father was referring to and said, "Oh, you mean—"

Her father cut her off. "Yes. There's nothing in the papers. No one here knows what's going on, because no one is writing about it."

"What about the shortwave radio?"

"That helps a bit, but those are foreign news services. I was hoping to see more American interest."

"Maybe no one here has time?"

"I think it's what we discussed before. There aren't enough economic interests there to be a major news story."

In the news, they had heard about the Korean Air plane that

had been shot down, killing everyone on board, and they'd heard President Reagan talk about the newly available Global Positioning System, but there was never anything in the news about the thousands of minorities in Sri Lanka who had been killed, or the tens of thousands of people that had been displaced, or the war that had broken out.

"I am glad you bought the shortwave radio," Maya said. "At least you get some news from your home country."

Maya had learned from her research that there were a few news outlets in the country reporting the ongoing events in Sri Lanka, but only in one or two large major US city newspapers. It wasn't easy for someone in a suburb like this one, where the nearest town of any size was Somerset, to hear about it.

"Aaaagh…" Maya's father said, putting his hand to his head. "People used to get along there, you know."

"What do you mean? It seems like there have been problems for a long time."

"In my childhood, people who spoke different languages, who practiced different religions, used to get along. We were neighborhood friends. We schooled together. We played together. We visited each other's homes," her father said. "We could be the best of friends, before the politicians got involved."

"I don't understand why dividing the country against itself helped the politicians, though. I've never understood that."

"The politicians needed a platform to win, I suppose. They needed to get groups of people to vote for them."

"Uh huh," Maya said. "I get that. But I still don't understand how turning people against their neighbors does that."

"Sometimes creating an enemy is an easy way to distract people from other issues. Like poverty or unemployment, for example. Once you've identified this supposed enemy, then you focus your energy on blaming that group for everything that is wrong and ignore that people are impoverished or unemployed. It's a tactic used in every country around the world."

"So they made the minority groups the enemy so people would overlook other problems?"

Her father nodded. "Perhaps, yes. And then they offered a solution to these so-called problems of poverty and unemployment by oppressing the minority groups through one language policies in order to lift up the others. But even the Indian prime minister has recognized that what happened in July was a genocide against the Tamils."

Somehow, putting the word "genocide" around it helped Maya grasp the gravity of the situation they'd experienced with even more clarity, but she still didn't understand how people like Vik, the man who'd been a longtime friend of her father's sister, could be so easily led to do horrible things to his fellow countrymen and women. Had people so quickly forgotten that, in the past, they'd all gotten along?

ALONE

Over the years, Maya had been forced to come to terms with the personal loneliness she had felt as an outsider in the US, and now she was grappling with the institutional loneliness she felt trying to fight for the innocent people left behind in her small, overlooked birth country. Kelsie and Sister Lucy had been like steady rocks in the stream of uncertainty gushing through her life and had really helped Maya feel less lonely in high school, but now she felt herself backsliding, isolated by having gone through something horrible that only her father could truly understand. She decided to go see Kelsie again, to see if maybe telling Kelsie a bit more about what had happened would help.

"C'mon. Let's go to the kitchen and have a snack," Kelsie said when Maya came in her front door. "Tell me what's going on, and I'll update you on what my dad has found out so far."

Kelsie's kitchen never failed to stop Maya in her tracks. It was so organized. Everything was spotless and had a place on the countertop: a toaster, a coffee pot, a plant, a dish rack next to the kitchen sink. Maya could barely find a plate and a fork when she needed one at home, and her kitchen was so foreign—with crocheted potholders and batik throw pillows, and the constant citrus scent of freshly brewed Ceylon tea, still referred to as "Ceylon" tea even after the country changed its name to Sri Lanka in 1972. They didn't even have a toaster. If you wanted toast, you put it on a baking sheet under the broiler.

Kelsie opened the freezer door and pulled a box out of it. She pulled two round waffles out of the box and popped them into the toaster, then opened her refrigerator and grabbed a plate.

Maya was amazed by how independent Kelsie was and always had been. It made her feel as immature and sheltered as a newborn bird in its nest.

"Kels, you never have to hunt for anything in your kitchen. Things are so organized here!"

Kelsie smiled. When the toaster popped, she opened up a cabinet door near the sink and pulled out two plates and put them down on the counter. Then she grabbed the two waffles out of the toaster and put one on each plate, covering them with the brownish-yellow substance she'd gotten from the refrigerator.

Maya examined the plate Kelsie handed her closely. "What is this combination, Kels?"

"Waffles with brown cheese," Kelsie replied, sitting down at the kitchen table. "Or something like brown cheese, anyway."

Maya poked at the waffle with a fork. "Oh. That's interesting. I've never heard of that combination."

"I love it. It seems weird, but it's one of my favorite snacks. Try it," Kelsie said.

Maya tried it. "This is actually really good!"

"Thanks. My grandparents introduced me to it when I was younger," Kelsie said between bites. "I guess it's something they eat in Norway." She set her fork down. "There's a whole Norwegian community around here, actually. I mean, not too many people, but a few people between here and Maryland. We get together with them sometimes."

"That's great. I didn't know there were any international communities here."

"Yeah, maybe not as many as before, I guess. And Norwegians kind of blend in with the Americans."

ALONE

Maya sat quietly, chewing on her waffle and thinking how nice it would be to be able to blend in.

"You're awfully quiet," Kelsie said. "What are you thinking about?"

"I'm just frustrated, I guess. I don't really know how to get somebody to pay attention to what's happening in Sri Lanka. And every day, I'm reminded of the thousands of people that were killed, of the innocent civilians still being killed."

"Thousands of people? You didn't tell me that before. That's huge, Maya."

"It's something I still think someone needs to get in front of our Congresspeople. Or, I guess *I* need to. I've written some letters to our government representatives, and I'm hoping to get some help requesting a meeting, but I don't think it will be enough," Maya said, shaking her head. "No. I *know* letters are not going to be enough."

Kelsie put her hand on top of Maya's hand. "Maya, you know you can't solve all the world's problems, right? I'm worried that you feel responsible for making this better."

"I *do* feel responsible," Maya said. "I mean, it happened to me and my dad! It's not something I just read about, you know? We were right there. And now, if I don't do something… I don't know how to live with myself. I wish I could just close my eyes and forget all about it, and believe me, I've tried, but I can't."

Kelsie was silent.

"Remember what Sister Lucy always told us? That helping other people was the most important thing you could do? Well, there are people who really need my help, but I just can't seem to figure out how to actually *do* anything."

Kelsie sighed. "Well, I got some ideas from my dad. But there must be other people like you, here and in other countries, trying to raise awareness, no?"

87

"I don't know. I haven't heard anything, and my father reads the news and listens to the radio all the time and he says almost no one talks about it here."

"There must be some way we can find other people who care. My father suggested trying to form a coalition of some sort," Kelsie added.

"I don't even know how to get started," Maya said, throwing her hands up. "How am I supposed to find people who care?"

"Oh Maya…" Kelsie let out a sigh of sympathy. "I know you're frustrated. Dad also suggested you contact Congress, but I told him you were already doing that."

"I also went to see Sister Lucy, to see whether she knew any charitable organizations on the ground that could help, or if the dioceses there could help."

"How was she?" Kelsie asked. "Was she doing well? Was she helpful?"

"Yeah, she's doing well. The crisis center hasn't changed a bit since we worked there. Sister Lucy told me to speak to that philosophy professor again," Maya said. "To help with stress. Do you remember him? The professor I spoke to in high school?"

"Vaguely," Kelsie said, scratching her head. "So have you reached out?"

"Not yet. I'm feeling a bit…ashamed, I guess. I feel like I should be handling this better. He tried to help me in the past, and now it just feels weird to ask for help again." She was quiet for a minute. "Did you know he used to be a Buddhist monk?"

Kelsie shook her head. "No. But I would take Sister Lucy's advice and really think about reaching out. I think it's a good idea. It doesn't have to be this minute. You can do it whenever you're ready."

Maya nodded and was silent for a few minutes. Then she looked up.

"Kelsie, I know it sounds crazy, but I can't just sit here while all this is happening. I am even starting to wonder…" Maya stopped mid-sentence and slapped her hand over her mouth.

"What? Tell me," Kelsie said.

"I'm thinking I should go back to Sri Lanka… I know, I know! It's a crazy idea. But so many people, including my relatives, are still stuck there."

"Wouldn't that be terribly dangerous?"

"I could wait for a quell in the fighting…"

Kelsie shook her head vehemently. "Listen to what you're saying, Maya! There's a war going on! You can't go back there."

Kelsie's mom came into the kitchen then and looked back and forth between her daughter and Maya.

"It looks like you girls are discussing something serious," she said, then gave Maya a hug. "I don't want to interrupt. Maya, why don't you join us for dinner later at the club?"

Maya said yes, never having laid eyes on the inside of a country club. She didn't know what to expect, other than she would be underdressed if she didn't go home to change.

#

When Maya got back to Kelsie's house, they piled into the car with Kelsie's parents and headed to the country club. Maya leaned toward Kelsie in the back seat and told her she'd been researching the logistics of a possible trip to Washington, D.C.

"I even called Jeev," Maya admitted. "He is in D.C. now at a law firm. A firm that also does some lobbying, I think."

"Jeev? The guy a few years ahead of us at school? Maya, wasn't he…?"

"What?"

"I just don't know if he's the type to care about helping?"

"What do you mean?"

"You remember how he was in high school?"

"Yes, definitely. But people grow up, right?"

"I don't know if Jeev did!"

"What do you mean?"

"I heard he came from a tough home background. And I don't know… I just heard things around school. He used to drink a lot, I do know that."

Maya recalled the phone call at the crisis center when the caller, who'd sounded suspiciously like Jeev, had admitted to drinking every day.

"Oh, and I thought of something else," Kelsie said. "Actually, Dad did. What do you think of sending a letter to the editor? You know, asking for more coverage of international news?"

"That sounds like a good idea to me."

"It's worth trying, right?"

When they arrived at the country club, Maya and Kelsie walked inside behind Kelsie's parents. It was the fanciest place Maya had ever been, decorated for fall with pumpkins and garlands of colored leaves and beautiful flower arrangements. The tables and chairs were fancy, and the cutlery was beautiful and shiny, and everything matched perfectly. Maya noticed how beautifully Kelsie's crushed velvet blouse and silk skirt matched their surroundings, even with her triple pierced ears.

Maya thought they would go straight to their table, but instead, Maya and Kelsie's parents joined the throng of adults who were milling around, cocktails in hand. The men patted each other on the back and the women chatted and everyone seemed so pleased to be there in their elegant clothes.

Kelsie's mother introduced Kelsie and Maya to a few of her friends, and Kelsie's father did the same, putting an arm around Kelsie like they were casual friends as he sang her praises. Maya smiled and said hello, but she felt awkward standing slightly off to the side, and she was sure her dress wasn't right. Kelsie must have noticed, because she suggested they go on a walk outside.

There was a beautiful big lawn and a pool that was unusually large behind the main building, and the water was such a clean shade of aqua blue that Maya was tempted to dive in. She wished again that she were a confident swimmer.

There was some sort of game in progress outside, a hunt for a hidden object, and Kelsie suggested that she and Maya participate as a team. They gathered with the rest of the crowd at the clubhouse. A tall man in a brown sweater and white collared shirt was instructing the participants where they could and could not search, and then he finally explained what they were hunting: a decorated log. People started wandering around the club's lawn looking for the log. The club grounds were vast, and Maya and Kelsie were both uncertain where to look, and so just wandered aimlessly like everyone else. After several minutes of searching, a man yelled out that he had found the log.

He carried the log back to the crowd, which had gathered again near the pool. When he placed the log in the center of the crowd, everyone said "Oooooh!" and "Aaaaah!" like he'd found something really valuable, and some people even started clapping.

The man in the brown sweater and white shirt shot his hand up to settle the crowd. "Congratulations! Well done. We do have a winner," he said, and everyone applauded.

People surrounded the winner and asked questions about how he'd known where to search. Maya stood back, struck by how trivial and inconsequential that evening's activities were. Did these people have a clue how lucky they were to spend an evening being so frivolous? And yet, the lightness and joy and lack of worry that the club members felt was something everyone should be able to feel.

Maya returned home after dinner and was struck by how plain their house was. The furniture, sourced from thrift stores over the years, was not fancy. There wasn't any wallpaper on the walls, much less framed art. The dishes in the dish rack next to the sink, picked up at garage sales, did not match. The cutlery on the dish rack was from at least a dozen different sets. The drinking glasses were few, and some had childish cartoon characters on them, while others were formal and out of place in the rack.

Maya sighed as she shut off the kitchen light. She knew she should be grateful. She had a safe place to live with proper western toilets and functioning indoor plumbing, food on the table in a calm and stable town, and a chance to get educated without being harassed. Things so many people in Sri Lanka could only dream about.

TRUST

When Jeev called in the late fall, Maya was astonished that he had remembered to call her. She'd been at a standstill over what else she could do and who she should consult when it came to bringing government attention to Sri Lanka, so she was happy to get his call, but also apprehensive. With Jeev, she never knew what to expect. She felt her gut punching at her from inside with a resounding question: *Could she trust him?*

Jeev's aggressive behavior during his senior year of high school was all too memorable, but Maya's disdain had been tempered with remembering that he was one of the only other students in school that looked different, just like her. For this reason alone, she thought he would be interested in what she had witnessed. He could sympathize with people who were persecuted just for being different.

They arranged to meet just outside their old high school. Maya arrived ten minutes early and walked around the grounds, looking for Jeev but also trying to shed some of her anxiety about seeing him. As she began another lap around the school, she heard Jeev's voice from a distance, piercing in the slightly frigid late autumn air.

"Hey, Maya! Have a seat here with me."

He was sitting on a bench. Seeing him reminded her of the men who had attacked her the past summer and Maya suddenly felt on edge. She hesitated to approach the bench, wondering whether agreeing to this rendezvous had been a huge mistake.

"Just a minute," Maya called out. She took her hands out of her coat pockets and clasped them together and puffed into them to warm them up. "Think," she said to herself. "Am I making a mistake? Am I inviting the proverbial devil to dinner?"

Maya rationalized away the discomfort she was feeling by reminding herself that she had called Jeev only to try to get help for others. And she had no intention of being completely rude now, especially since she had initiated their reconnection. So, she plodded along toward the benches, setting aside her discomfort and wariness.

Jeev hadn't changed. Even more than before, he resembled others she had known in her father's community. He wore a beguiling grin, which was typical of Jeev, who had always had a disarming expression on his face. He'd used it to his advantage in high school, feigning innocence whenever anyone accused him of wrongdoing.

He had his hands shoved in his coat pockets and was slouching on the bench with his legs wide open.

"Hey there," Jeev said.

"Hi," Maya said, trying to quiet the butterflies in her stomach. "Thanks for remembering to call."

"Sure, yeh, whatever. Why don't you sit down?" Jeev said. "It's been ages."

"Yes, it has," Maya said, taking a seat and leaving as much distance between them as she could on the bench.

"What have you been up to?"

"Oh, you know, college, travel, the usual," Maya said. "How about you?"

"Well, I finished college in D.C. a few years ago and then I stayed down there to work. But I guess you knew that somehow."

"I heard…from Kelsie," Maya said

"Oh yes, your friend Kelsie," Jeev said, as if he knew a secret about Kelsie.

"So how are things in D.C.?" Maya asked.

"I interned at a law firm and ended up staying on as a paralegal," he said, shrugging. "No big deal. Eventually I'll apply to law school."

"I thought Kelsie said you worked for a lobbying firm?"

"My firm does some lobbying, yes. Most all the firms in D.C. do."

"Oh, I see," Maya said. "I guess I didn't know that."

"So what do you do?"

"I'm actually applying to graduate school now and working in a temporary position nearby while I wait to hear back."

"Interesting," Jeev said, without probing further. He was quiet for a few moments, then added, "You know, I've always wondered, where are you from? I heard you might be from the same place as my father."

"Really?" Maya asked. "I wanted to talk to you about that, actually. I was born in Sri Lanka. And my father and brothers and I went back there this summer, and…something happened. And I thought maybe it might help the people there, the people who were affected, if I could speak to someone in government."

"*Something* happened? What kind of something?"

"Something troubling." Over the next few minutes, Maya explained what she had witnessed while tolerating Jeev's questions and asides, which went off topic several times. She was wondering if he had just never developed much in the way of etiquette or social graces when she noticed the annoyed look on his face.

"Jeev, are you ok?" Maya asked.

"Why are we here, Maya?"

"Because there are people in trouble. You said your father is from Sri Lanka, right? There's a war going on there, and discrimination that has been going on for decades, and I thought I would run it by you, in case you might want to help, or your law firm could help. I don't know anyone else in Washington…"

"Help?" Jeev sneered. "What am I supposed to do? And why should I?"

Before Maya could respond, Jeev launched into a tirade, accusing her of being a bad person, of having abandoned him and their friendship in high school.

Maya listened, but her mind was in a whirl. She had never really thought of Jeev as a close friend. In fact, they had hardly spoken to each other in high school, outside of a few times at school newspaper meetings. They had never confided anything in each other. Where was he getting this, about Maya abandoning him?

Maya didn't know which was more alarming—Jeev's tirade, or the fact that once it was delivered, he calmed down and picked up the conversation where it had been left off. He told Maya that his father had recently traveled to Washington, D.C. with other prominent businessmen, attorneys, physicians, and professors to meet with a group of Congressmen who had agreed to listen to their stories about the atrocities in Sri Lanka.

"My father's actually been in contact with several MPs in Britain also, trying to appeal to their interests in the extended British Commonwealth," he said.

"He knows members of Parliament?"

Jeev nodded.

"Wait—so your father already knows all about what's happening? And you know?" Maya asked.

"Yeah, I know," Jeev responded dryly. "We're Tamil."

"You're Tamil, too?"

"Yes, Maya," Jeev said, rolling his eyes. "Duh."

Then why was he being so hostile if they had this in common, if he knew about the suffering happening in Sri Lanka? What was he so angry about?

"Tell me more about his trip to D.C.," Maya said gently. "Has your father been back to Sri Lanka? How does he know what's going on?"

"He knows some people over there trying to help the minority cause. He's been working with some groups."

"Do you mean one of the insurg–err, freedom fighter groups?" Maya asked.

"You were going to say insurgent groups, weren't you?"

Maya didn't respond.

"You know, they are the only people trying to do something for the civilians that have been left behind. They are fighting for their freedom and equality," Jeev said.

"I'm not trying to pass judgment. I just don't know much about those groups. I thought there was some disagreement among the different groups, right?" Maya asked, swallowing back a lump in her throat.

Jeev's expression was icy.

"Can you tell me more? I am genuinely curious," she said calmly.

"I can't say more. It's private," Jeev said sternly. "My father wouldn't like me talking about it."

Maya thought about Jeev's father for a moment and the call she had received at the hotline one night when she thought the voice at the other end was Jeev.

"Is everything okay with you and your father?" she asked.

"That's none of your business," Jeev snapped. Then he said, "I don't suppose you've ever met with a Congressman? Or anyone from a high stakes group?"

"No, but I hope to have the chance in the near future," Maya said.

Jeev laughed. "Really? You?"

Maya forced herself to take a deep breath before answering. "Yes, I have written some letters, and I'm hoping to get an in-person meeting. Someone my father knows might help us host. Hopefully it happens, because things are really bad over there."

"You're so naive, Maya," Jeev said, then continued before Maya could come up with a response. "You have to have influence. You're a nobody. Who's going to meet with some girl fresh out of college just because she saw something that bothered her while she was on vacation?"

"That's not at all—" Maya started to explain but stopped when she felt Jeev's hand on her thigh.

"If you stick with me, spend more time with me, I can help you understand how things work in the real world," Jeev said, rubbing her leg. "I can show you how to get results."

Maya pushed his hand away and started to get up from the bench, but Jeev grabbed her arm and held her there, laughing.

"I always liked you, Maya," he said. "We could—"

Maya didn't let him finish. She pulled her arm out of his grasp and said, "This is not how people who like each other act."

"What are you talking about?" Jeev said. "You asked for my help, and I'm giving it to you. I'm telling you I always *liked* you, Maya. You should be flattered."

"So you think you can use your father's money and status to take advantage of me?" she clapped back. As soon as the words left her mouth, Maya regretted saying them. She knew she had hit a sore spot with Jeev, whose face was now full of fury.

"You don't know anything about my father!" Jeev snarled. "You know what, Maya? You're just a nobody. A naive, stupid girl with no influence and no connections."

Maya began to walk away, but Jeev wasn't finished.

"Nobody will ever listen to you," he said to her back. "You will never matter."

"Well, maybe people like you and your father just need to throw money around because there's nothing else about you that's impressive," she said. "Look, I'm leaving. I'm sorry I called you. I don't know who you are anymore." She began walking away, as quickly as possible.

"You can't walk away from me! I'm the only person who will bother to help you."

Maya could hear him get up and could feel him start to follow her. Maya turned to see Jeev closing in on her and she began to run, back towards the school building. Jeev caught her arm and pressed her against the brick wall of the school and Maya could feel the prickly pieces of brick pressing into her back.

Jeev clenched his fist, and Maya gasped and moved her head to avoid the blow, closing her eyes against what was coming. She felt a sharp pain on her left shoulder and opened her eyes. Jeev had punched her shoulder, hard, against the brick wall. He lifted his hand, ready to hit her again, but Maya ducked, and his fist connected with the brick wall.

As Jeev bent over his bleeding fist, Maya ducked under his arm and ran down the asphalt path to the nearest door. She opened it and thrust herself inside.

She was out of breath, and her left shoulder was throbbing. She was in shock that someone she knew had punched her in broad daylight, in public, for no apparent reason. She didn't expect that sort of thing here, in a quiet American suburb.

#

It had been an unusually awful and eventful long morning. Before leaving the school, Maya had poked her head outside to make sure Jeev was nowhere in sight, and then she had set out for home, with her shoulder throbbing in pain. She walked as if in a trance, her hand pressing against her shoulder to try to clamp down on the pain, tears streaming down her cheeks.

She could feel the hot liquid of her tears on her face, dripping down her cheeks and chin and onto the arm she was holding close against her body. She hoped no one could see she was crying. Of course, she didn't need to worry about Mr. Haggerty, who hadn't cared when she was attacked by a dog and surely wouldn't care that someone had punched her.

She reached home and was relieved her father wasn't there to confront her about what had happened while she tended to her shoulder, rummaging in the bathroom drawers for hydrogen peroxide and antibiotic ointment. She didn't want to talk about what had happened with Jeev with anyone, so she forced those thoughts out of her mind and focused on what she had learned from the conversation before it turned ugly.

She put a Band-Aid on her wound and then turned on the television set to see what else was transpiring in the world. The Queen of England was on a public channel documentary, which wasn't exactly a distraction. Instead, it made her think how funny it was that so many former British colonies wanted to remain a part of the British Commonwealth. Or maybe it wasn't that they wanted to, but rather that they needed to? Sri Lanka, after all, had chosen to remain a part of the British Commonwealth, too, no doubt for the political and economic support.

The US, however, had fully broken free after 1776, and grown strong and big and powerful. It had also tried to give people freedom to just be, to pursue their own paths. Here the people could keep the government in check, at least in theory.

Maya slumped on the couch, her thoughts running wild in her head. The promise of the US, the inner workings of Washington, D.C., Jeev's physical attack. What if she had made a mistake in reaching out to Jeev? It was bad enough he'd attacked her and said horrible things, but what if he got his father involved somehow?

Maya felt momentarily dizzy. She wondered how the conversation would go if she told Sister Lucy what had transpired. Maya wasn't sure whether Sister Lucy would encourage her to go to the authorities about another former student, or simply advise Maya to put that behind her and focus on the task at hand. "What's done is done," Maya imagined her saying. "Now let's think about how we can do better moving forward."

On top of how terrible she felt about the encounter with Jeev, Maya was troubled at the claims and revelations Jeev had made around his father's trip to Washington, D.C., and especially around the inner workings of influence there. *How difficult was it really going to be to get something done without money?*

And Maya didn't know what to make of Jeev's confession about his father's possible connection with some of the freedom fighting groups. Again, she wondered if she had made a huge and irreversible mistake reaching out to him.

STUCK

As an island country, Sri Lanka had always been physically isolated from the rest of the world, and Maya had grown up with a sense of what that physical isolation meant as her teachers pointed to tiny Sri Lanka underneath India on her classroom's pull-down map. But in Maya's new home in America, she felt emotionally isolated; something she couldn't quite explain or point to on a map. That feeling had intensified since she'd returned from her birth country. With war unfolding and the humanitarian crisis intensifying back in Sri Lanka while loved ones and other innocent people remained trapped, the isolation and uncertainty of being unable to help was agonizing. And this uncertainty gave new meaning to the limbo Maya had always felt growing up, not fitting in any one place, as if she was living in a no man's land. At times she felt like she was simply bending and morphing to try to fit into her surroundings with no real success, not really ever belonging anywhere.

Now with winter and the holidays approaching, Maya hoped that there would be a reprieve from the barrage of recent unpleasantries. Right now, she needed a reminder of the things she looked forward to in the US. Christmas had always held a particular fascination for Maya, especially after she had met Kelsie and Sister Lucy. The lavish displays of lights on neighborhood homes that she would see as she walked in their neighborhoods with Kelsie, the trees festooned with beautiful ornaments she saw out shopping with her brothers during their visits home, the joyful sounds of Christmas music and carolers Sister Lucy loved, the sweet smell of hot chocolate with marshmallows melting in mugs her father would prepare, and the excitement of putting on some ice skates with Kelsie—these were all sights and sounds and smells and experiences Maya welcomed with enthusiasm once she had Kelsie, and then Sister Lucy, to share them with.

But unlike Kelsie, whose house seemed to overflow with aunts and uncles and cousins during the holidays, Maya had hardly any contact with relatives, not even during the holidays. She had also never even met any of her father's work colleagues over the years. Sometimes, however, they would see her father's old family friends from Sri Lanka, the Swami family and the Fernandes family, and a few others.

"*Machan*, it's great to see you," the men would say, greeting Maya's father in the affectionate term reserved for someone close. These families had also arrived in America several years back, and were making their way in this new world, just like Maya's family. The wives would whisper among themselves, and share recipes, and update each other on their children during these holiday visits, and Maya would be forced to sit among the women and children while her brothers were welcomed into the conversations between her father and the other men.

These other Sri Lankan families and children were scattered across different towns and schools, but they lived within two- or three-hours' drive, and so continued to make the effort to get together every few years during holidays. But none of the guests were more than casual friends, and Maya didn't feel that she really knew any of them. If their children were to attend the same school, Maya suspected they would hardly acknowledge her. She did know them well enough, though, to know that the Swami family was Tamil and the Fernandes family was Sinhalese.

STUCK

"Maya, back home everyone got along for many decades, despite speaking different languages or coming from different religious backgrounds. We also had friends from the Sri Lankan Burgher community," her father told her when he announced they'd host a holiday party that year. Burghers were part Dutch or British, a vestige of the colonialism that was the reality of a pre-1948 Sri Lanka, which was called Ceylon then. The Portuguese had been in Sri Lanka since 1505, then the Dutch in 1658, and then the British in 1798. These loose friendships of her father's in America represented the gamut of Sri Lankan colonial history.

During these holiday visits, they always made *sambol*, a spicy condiment that required scraping a coconut with the tableside scraping tool. "Maya, step back so that your fingers don't get near the serrated blade," her father would say as he wound the tool around and around the inside of the coconut. The sambol was accompanied by string hoppers, vermicelli noodles firmly shaped into nests, which one family usually contributed for the luncheon. This was always followed by a festive Sri Lankan cake another family would bring with them.

"Oh, how beautifully and meticulously you've decorated it with so many shapes and flowers, *Rani*," the women would joke, referring to one another as "queen" and digging their forks into the thick buttercream frosting in four different colors—green, blue, red, and yellow. Sometimes the cake would be the Sri Lankan Christmas cake, a modified version of the British and American fruit cakes, and Maya could not get enough of that.

"Aunty, is this rose water and cardamom I smell?" she would ask, crunching on the cashews while the cake melted in her mouth.

"Oliver, man..." the men would say during these infrequent gatherings, and then slap her father on the back or shoulder as they drank and told jokes. Maya didn't know what the men discussed, only that the conversations involved hushed tones and the occasional outburst of laughter.

It had been like this for years. Maya and her family would see these other Sri Lankan families only occasionally, never sharing anything personal together. There were no deep conversations; they did not confide in one another. They did not get close, though Maya would have welcomed this. Just casual company over casual food, over some holiday or Christmas gatherings, seemingly with a goal of maintaining some loose tether to their old culture.

Their interactions reminded Maya of the challenges the adults in the group had adapting to American culture, and simultaneously underscored how that contrasted with the desires of the children in the group to be accepted by their American friends and counterparts. The adults celebrated their vague memories of Tamil culture, but that was combined with post-Victorian cultural restraint, creating an odd mix that made it more difficult for the children to break free and be truly American or accepted.

Now Maya just yearned for warmth. She didn't want to think about those cold Christmases spent with her father's acquaintances; she wanted familiar Christmas music and hot cocoa, and to be rid of the angst she was still feeling as her future, and the future of the people in Sri Lanka, hung in the balance.

As Maya sat at the kitchen table, prodding her sore shoulder with her fingers, she checked the time. Kelsie had called Maya early that morning to tell her that Sister Lucy had organized Christmas carol singing around town.

"My father will pick you up, too, if you want, and drive us to the first caroling site," Kelsie said.

When Maya mentioned it to her father before leaving to meet Kelsie, he'd said, "Remember to come back on time. I need to call my cousin to check on him and I know he'll want to hear your voice, too."

"Your cousin?" Maya asked, wondering whether her father felt lonely over the holidays.

"Yes, my second cousin. The one whose father was killed in the 1977 riots."

"I don't think you ever told me about that?"

"His father was killed in front of him. One of the rioters slit his throat with a machete," Maya's father said. "So I call to check on him."

Maya was shocked. She couldn't imagine witnessing your own father's murder. What had happened to her grandmother's maid was horrible enough, but your own father? It was unthinkable.

"He's had a lot of stress and physical issues. I've been checking up on him over the years…" her father said, his voice trailing off.

"Is he okay?"

"Well, at first none of us talked to him about it, because we didn't want to dredge up horrific memories for him… But then he started having chronic dizzy and fainting spells and started to feel scared walking around."

"That's terrible," Maya said, thinking that she understood far better than she wished she did.

Maya's father stared into his teacup before continuing. "He told us he felt a blanket of anxiety and fear suffocating him every time he went anywhere. Even inside his own house. He has had trouble sleeping, too. He had to retire on disability."

"And where is he now?"

"In Canada, but he has a brother outside Chicago and so he spends time in both places so his brother can look after him. I'm going to call him at his brother's place to check on him, especially now with the holidays approaching. It's a particularly difficult time when you have lost someone."

Maya nodded, wondering if her father was actually speaking about her mother. Then she pushed the thought away and left to get ready for caroling. She quickly changed her clothes and was trying to ease her sore shoulder into her winter coat when Kelsie's father honked from the driveway.

When Kelsie's father dropped them off in front of a church downtown, they saw a crowd waiting in the parking lot and went to join them. Maya gathered the sides of her coat together and hugged her body with it as she started walking. Her teeth were chattering in the icy wind, and she had forgotten gloves. As they joined the group, Maya looked around but did not recognize any of the adults leading the carols.

Eventually someone started handing out candles and sheet music. The pages flapped in the wind as Maya looked over the music. She recognized most of the songs—standard Christmas carols like "Away in the Manger" and "Silent Night"—but there were a few she did not recognize. A man with brown curly hair and horn-rimmed glasses lifted his hand in the air and motioned for the group to gather around him. He instructed everyone on the order of songs and where they would go in town. At each place they would stop, they would repeat the small repertoire of songs.

They practiced a few songs in the parking lot, the man with brown curly hair waving his hands to conduct the group. Then they lit the candles that were handed out. Some people, anticipating the wind, had brought flashlights.

Maya relished the sound of the music. It was peaceful, harmonious, soft, soothing, a welcome light in the December darkness and chill, as well as the twisted and macabre journey in which she currently found herself. She didn't want the singing to stop.

As the music took hold of her, Maya forgot about the disarray that the past summer had brought into her life. She forgot about the fire and the people that were killed in the hospital and about the mob attacks and having to hide out for days in a refugee camp with little food and water. She forgot about their narrow escape from Sri Lanka, and about Jeev's aggressive comments and assault. She simply reveled in the beautiful sound of the music.

"I am with you," a voice said directly in Maya's ear.

Maya looked around for the source of the voice, which sounded exactly like the professor's voice that had come to her in the stairwell when she and her father were running from the mobs.

At first, Maya didn't see an obvious source for the voice, but then her eyes settled on a man to her right with gentle eyes. Was it really him, the philosophy professor, singing carols with them? She called out, "Professor, is that you?" not caring who heard her.

The man moved closer next to her and whispered, "Maya, it's time for you to call me again. Or come and see me. There is something weighing heavy in your mind."

At first, the professor's nearness made her stiffen up, remembering both the man who'd been prepared to rape her and Jeev's violence. But then she remembered she wasn't alone, and that Kelsie was with her.

"How did you know I was here, professor?" Maya asked.

Kelsie turned to see what was going on.

"I spoke to Sister Lucy," he said. "She told me you would be here this evening."

Maya kept telling herself to remain calm, that she had spoken to this man previously, that he had been introduced to her by Sister Lucy. Maya nodded to him and tried to find her place in the sheet music.

Kelsie nudged Maya. "Who was that man?" she whispered against the whistle of the wind.

"Do you remember that philosophy professor that Sister Lucy introduced me to?" Maya said quietly, trying to hold on to her music.

She turned back to speak to the professor again, to introduce him to Kelsie, but he was no longer standing next to her. She searched for him among the carolers, but he was nowhere to be seen. He had disappeared.

PART THREE

"Life begins on the other side of despair."
—Jean-Paul Sartre

DISCOVERY

Things were progressing with Jase. Maya was enjoying their deepening friendship and budding romance, but some mornings she still sat in her bed and stared at the ceiling, feeling dejected, unsure if she wanted to get out of bed. It dawned on her finally that she needed to try to resolve things in her past if she was going to move forward. Obviously brushing things under the rug wasn't working, nor was focusing solely on what she could do to help others instead of fixing her own issues.

The memories and guilt continued to push their way through and emit their silent cries for help, and Maya couldn't ignore them any longer. So, she finally took Sister Lucy's suggestion and began seeing a therapist. She felt compelled to give this a try first, before attempting to reach out to the professor, the former monk, again, especially because she still didn't understand how he'd just materialized at her side during the carol singing.

Maya walked downtown from her father's home once a week to visit the therapist's office. He was a stocky man with a square jaw and slicked-back, graying hair who wore a dull brown suit each time she saw him. At first she would sit quietly and answer the therapist's questions, which were followed by long episodes of silence. Sometimes both the questions and silence bored her, so she would look around the therapist's room, but even that didn't help much. The room was dark and drab, not happy or joyous in any way, and the chair she sat in was brown, with flat rectangular cushions, and a deep back, made for a large man and far too big for Maya. Or she would stare at his slicked back hair to see whether any strands were out of place that day. Anything to distract herself from the awkward silences.

Maya felt uncomfortable being open about her experiences, embarrassed to be completely open with an older man whom she did not know. How could he possibly understand what she had been through? How could he possibly understand what it felt like to be singled out and chased by murderous mobs because you were of a different race, a different religion, a different gender? How could he possibly understand what it felt like to come here from a small country that very few people had heard of, for which very few shared concern? How could he possibly understand how it felt to be invisible and ignored? How could he possibly understand how challenging it was to adapt and assimilate to a new place? So, she shared very little each week.

Therapy felt like a waste of time for Maya, like she was checking off a box so that she could say she had tried. Still, she kept returning to the therapist's office, hoping he could help her excavate the inner recesses of her mind, hoping something the therapist would do or say would make a difference. On one of her visits, he asked her to share what she was thinking about at that very moment.

"I've been thinking about the paradox of discrimination," Maya began.

"What do you mean? Tell me more," the therapist said.

"I have witnessed discrimination among the people of my father's and grandfather's ethnic community, in my birth country. And I have been harassed by people, too, in my own birth country. Those are communities I was born into but left when we moved to America. And those communities stratify things like skin color, social status, and marriage. Being part American, it was hammered into me by relatives growing up how 'lucky' I was to be 'lighter-skinned' than them… But still, I was a minority in my own country, and here, I am still different. I don't quite fit in anywhere," Maya said.

"Hmmm…" the therapist gazed attentively at Maya, his thumb and forefinger rubbing his chin. "How do you feel about that?"

"Well, at the core, I believe…"

"Yes? Go on."

"Well last year I had the opportunity to look at several possible graduate school opportunities. And for the first time, I had to seriously consider a move to another part of the country."

"Interesting. I'm not sure I understand, though. What were your concerns?"

"Well, I suddenly thought about my twin brothers in college. They've had a mixed experience growing up, an experience different from mine. They look even more different than I do, and it's been hard for them. They've experienced more outward discrimination than I have. So I wondered what would have happened if *they* had to be plucked from where they were and suddenly put down in another region of the country? Perhaps one that was less accustomed to people who looked different? How would they be treated on a day-to-day basis?" Maya suggested.

"Hmmm… What do you think about that, Maya?"

"Well, what do *you* think? I thought that was why I was here, to get advice from you."

"This is your time to speak. I'm here to listen."

Maya thought for a moment how she should respond. "Well, I am very grateful, despite the harrowing experiences of last summer, despite the minor transgressions here over the years, I'm very grateful to have made it out alive. To have been given the chance to live, despite the trying circumstances last summer, and experiences over the years… I'm grateful to be here, in America, I guess is what I'm saying."

And that was that. Over the following weeks, Maya ultimately found that nothing the therapist said or did made her feel better. She didn't even know if she was really healing, mainly because the therapist only kept pummeling her with questions each week. He never gave her advice about anything, never told her stories or gave her examples. He never actually engaged in any real dialogue with her.

Later Maya would learn that there were different types of therapists, and that some believed in just asking questions and doing nothing else. They were the type that thought that patients could talk and talk and talk and eventually answer their own questions. Still, even when she had that knowledge, Maya didn't revise her opinion of this therapist, who never asked any questions that made Maya think she was solving anything.

Finally Maya terminated her visits to the therapist, grateful, at least, that he had forced her to talk more openly to herself about what she had gone through, even though she still felt suspended in perpetual uncertainty.

#

Maya had not wanted to burden or taint her growing friendship with Jase with the horrific details of what had occurred the past summer. Not now. Not this early in what Maya hoped would turn into a real, and possibly intimate, relationship. So whenever Jase would return from Pittsburgh to visit his family, they took walks in town and shared stories about their childhoods. Jase was always respectful and seemed interested in what she had to say, and as they became more acquainted with one another, the awkwardness she felt around him began to dissipate.

There was one thing she remained nervous about, however: despite spending hours in each other's company, they'd never kissed, and Maya began to doubt whether they ever would. The longer it took for this milestone to occur, the more nervous Maya began to feel. She wondered whether Jase hesitated to take the next step because of their past together as school friends, or was he just being himself, an old-fashioned type of guy who was respectful and took it slow with girls? Part of her welcomed his slowness though, and the lack of sexual pressure of any sort.

They were walking back toward the swimming pool near their old high school, chatting about a new restaurant Jase had discovered in Pittsburgh, when suddenly Jase abruptly stopped on the pavement and said, "Maya, I think you're beautiful."

Maya felt her cheeks flush and immediately became flustered. She didn't know how to respond and simply said, "No one has ever said that to me before."

"Your eyes are beautiful."

Maya immediately looked away, embarrassed.

"Your hair is beautiful, too. I love the way it smells."

Maya's hand went instinctively to her hair.

"And I just love your gumption."

"Gumption?" Maya repeated, glad Jase didn't know how difficult it was some mornings for her to get out of bed.

"So, what are you going to do tonight?"

Maya thought about how mundane her evenings were. "The same as usual. Prep for work, do some reading, maybe even take up my flute again after all these years."

"You never told me you play the flute."

"Oh, I didn't? I guess it didn't come up."

"Can you play something for me sometime?"

"I need to brush up…but sure, sometime."

"I would really like that."

They walked in silence for a few more minutes. Maya was thinking about all those conversations with the therapist, and how good it had felt to open up a bit.

"You're quiet," Jase said to her, breaking the silence. "What are you thinking?"

Maya was overcome with a feeling she should take a chance. "Jase, I, uh…"

"Yes?"

"Hypothetically speaking…"

"Yes?"

"If I witnessed something horrible, unspeakable acts of violence, but it was in another country, do you think I should speak out to *our* government, here in the US? Do you think it can make a difference? I mean, do you think they'll care?"

Jase laughed abruptly. "Okay, that is not what I thought you were going to say." Then he grew serious. "I think so, yes. There are people in government, in the State Department, for instance, that keep track of things around the world, and try to manage American interests."

Jase always sounded so wise to Maya, but she wasn't sure he could fully appreciate the struggle of smaller countries.

"That's just it, though. I don't know if the US has any interests in the part of the world I was in."

"You should still say something, Maya," he said, turning to look at her as they walked. "Even if the government here can't do anything, it could catch the attention of others who might be interested to do something."

"Like who?" Maya asked.

"You know, journalists, or private citizens, or organizations. I've seen it happen before, when a protest gets a lot of attention, for instance. My uncle, he used to make things happen."

"Your uncle?" Maya asked.

"I had an uncle who became an activist," Jase continued. "He would write to his government representatives and show up to public meetings and forums and town halls to ask questions."

"Do you think anyone can do that? I mean, do you think our representatives even read letters from ordinary citizens?"

"I heard they read letters from everyone, at least their staff does. That's what my uncle said, anyway."

"Well, I've started to do some of that. I wrote to our government representatives, and I'm trying to get a meeting with them, fingers crossed."

"I'm intrigued. You're getting more interesting by the day, Maya."

"I am?"

"Yeah. What did you write about? Do you, umm, do you want to tell me what you saw?"

Maya hesitated at first. "I saw people being violently attacked. Thousands of people have died. I saw men getting their throats slit, and a woman thrown into a fire…" Maya felt herself getting choked up and swallowed back the lump in her throat.

"My God. That sounds gruesome," Jase said, stopping in his tracks, turning to look at Maya. "Are you okay?"

She turned to Jase. "I think so. They were coordinated attacks, and the government didn't do anything to stop them. In fact, they may have been involved. That's the really troubling thing. There's a history there of targeting ethnic minorities like my dad's…"

"Wait. Wait. Slow down," Jase said, stopping on the sidewalk and turning to Maya. "Where were you when this happened?"

"In Asia, in Sri Lanka. It's part of the British Commonwealth."

"And that's where you were born, right?"

"Yes. My dad is from there, but my mom was American. I'm part American, and a US citizen now."

"Did you grow up there?"

"In my early years. I don't remember too much. I came here at the beginning of middle school."

"Really? I didn't realize you only came in middle school," he said. "I guess I thought…well, I don't know what I thought. I just can't believe we never talked about any of this in high school."

"Why would we? We only saw each other in science class and on the forensics team."

Jase held out his arm for Maya to take and they resumed walking. "Well, I'm even more intrigued now. So, what did you write to the representatives about?"

"The violence there. The war. And the ongoing attacks on minorities."

"I'm sorry," Jase said, sighing. "I didn't know."

"That's okay, most people don't know. It never makes it into the mainstream news here. And I told them more about what happened to me and my father."

"Are you shaking, Maya?" Jase asked. He stopped and hugged her. "Are you okay?"

"I don't know. I think I just haven't processed it all yet," Maya said over his shoulder as he held her close.

Jase released her and looked at her. "You can talk to me about it if you want."

Maya said, "Thanks. But I haven't heard back from any of the representatives. I felt like I should say something, you know, and ask for help. I mean, for the people left behind, the people struggling there, if the government here would do anything, could do anything."

"So write to them again. Maybe they don't hear enough about it from enough people. You know they are probably busy. You should write again."

"Do you think so?"

"Absolutely, you should. And you should ask for a meeting. Don't just write. Don't just tell them what happened. Ask for a meeting. The more people that get this in front of them…" Jase grabbed Maya's hands and cupped them in his. "I can even help you if you want."

"Thank you. I mean that," Maya said. "I don't know anyone like you, Jase."

They continued to walk until they reached the swimming pool, which was covered up for winter. Maya looked at the pool and said, "Maybe I'll take you up on your offer to help me become a good swimmer. When it's warm, of course."

"I would like that," he said.

Maya felt giddy with the thought of spending more time with Jase as they passed the swimming pool and headed back in silence toward the building where they had begun.

This time it was Maya who broke the silence as they passed the benches just outside the school building. "What are you thinking about now?"

"Have we ever taken any pictures together? I don't think I have any photos of us."

"No. I guess not."

"I want you to have a picture of me, something to remember me by when we are not together," Jase said.

"Oh," Maya said, unsure how to respond.

"I have one…a photograph. I brought it just for you."

"You did?"

"Yes. I wrote my number on the back, too, so you don't forget me."

Jase took Maya to a quiet corner near the building and held her hands. Her back was against the brick wall, and she studied his face as he inched closer. His light brown eyelashes were just visible through the orange-rimmed sunglasses he was wearing, and Maya could smell Jase's skin as he inched closer. He smelled fresh, soapy and clean. Jase leaned in and kissed Maya. It felt like an eternity to her, but it was not really much more than a quick peck in the end.

Her first real adult kiss. That was all Maya could think about. Nothing sloppy like the few college boys she'd kissed in secret, wanting to explore what her father had forbidden for so many years. It felt amazing to her. She could not think about anything else in that moment. Her heart was pounding.

Then Jase looked at her, calm and collected, and cleared his throat.

Maya stood in a half daze, not fully internalizing anything he said after that.

"I'm going to need to head back to the gym, to the locker, to grab my bags," Jase said.

Maya felt a pit in her stomach. She knew this time of day would arrive, the time to say goodbye, but she didn't want this moment to end. She didn't want her afternoon with Jase to end. She simply said, "Uh huh."

"I'm glad we met all those years ago. Did I ever tell you that?" Jase said.

Maya stood silent for a moment. "Me, too," she said finally. It was silly, but she missed him already.

Jase put his hand in his pocket and pulled out his wallet. He flipped it open and pulled out a picture of himself and handed it to Maya.

Maya took the photo and looked at it. It was beautiful. It was a recent photo of Jase, capturing his kind eyes. She flipped over the photo and saw a phone number written diagonally in blue pen.

"That's my number. You can call me if you want when I'm in Pittsburgh. I know you said your dad was still uncomfortable with the idea of your dating. So we can just talk."

"I told you that about my dad?" Maya said. She had no clue how dating in America was supposed to happen, other than what she'd seen on television.

DISCOVERY

"Yeah. But I don't want to date anyone else, so if we can talk regularly, that will be great."

"Are we dating?" Maya blurted out.

"It doesn't matter to me what you call it. The only woman I want to talk to is you, Maya."

Maya grabbed Jase around the shoulders and then his neck and hugged him. She hadn't imagined she could feel this way about a man, especially after the attack in July and Jeev's violence, but Jase made her feel safe. He was respectful and honest, and she felt comfortable with him. It was all so unexpected, but also wonderful.

"Goodbye. See you tomorrow, maybe, before you leave?"

Maya watched him turn around and head back toward the gym.

BETRAYAL

"I can't believe what I'm hearing," her father's voice boomed from the family room, startling Maya, who was in her bedroom.

Then there was silence. Maya sat up from her bed, curious as to the cause of her father's annoyance.

"He stole approximately fifteen thousand dollars from me, a member of our own community," her father said.

It sounded as if her father was on the telephone.

"Rosie, you're right, we should try to forgive those who do not know better, but at his age, shouldn't he have known better? Isn't it a crime to steal? And more so from someone in your own community. I just don't think we're going to see eye to eye on this," her father said.

He was definitely on the phone, talking to his sister, Rosie. Maya walked into the kitchen as he was hanging up. Her father nodded at her, then headed toward the foyer, grabbing his raincoat from the closet.

"I am stepping out," he said, but then he paused in front of the front door, running his hand through his hair and sighing audibly. "I just cannot believe how fractured our community is, despite its small size."

Maya tried to think of something to calm down her father. She remembered her hotline training and thought acknowledging his feelings may help.

"I remember you saying something like that in the past," she said. "It must be frustrating."

Even though her father was half-British by ancestry, Maya knew he was speaking of the Sri Lankan community. In many ways, he identified more with that side of his heritage because he had been raised there. It had been his home, and his family's home. His mother had left England permanently to marry his father, and for her, too, Sri Lanka was cherished.

"You know, I could have taken the easy way out and washed my hands of all this. We're in America. We have a new life."

It was true, Maya thought. They could have both simply washed their hands of everything at this point, and maybe that would have been wise.

Her father continued, "How could someone from my own community do this to me?"

Maya didn't know what to make of these comments since he wasn't bothering to explain what had happened. But she had her own issue with the Sri Lankan community. Just last week she had discovered that Mrs. Fernandes had told some of the other Sri Lankan mothers that Maya had become soiled before marriage since she was dating, and a boy outside the community, no less. She told them that Maya was now unmarriageable, tainted. So much for a supportive, close-knit community.

Maya sighed and walked back to her room as her father left the house. She stared at the photo of Jase lying on top of her nightstand, and then flopped down on her bed. Mrs. Fernandes was a gossip, everyone knew that, but why would she target Maya and say such nasty things? Perhaps it was because Mrs. Fernandes and her daughter did not get along and she needed to take it out on someone. Maya had heard through the years that the Fernandes' daughter was fairly rebellious, that there were days during their childhood when she would even deliberately skip school.

Maya thought that strangers in a new land with something in common would support one another. But this had never really been the case, not with the Fernandes family or even with the Swami family. Perhaps it was emblematic of the problems the quotas had created, when people had to compete within their own community just to get opportunities. Maybe her father was right about the community being fractured. Maybe they'd brought that baggage with them when they came to America.

#

Maya glanced at her face in the mirror before sitting down at her desk to wait for her father, who was still getting dressed for the reception at the Swami family's house almost an hour away. She was dreading the reception, dreading coming face to face with the gossip Mrs. Fernandes had been spreading, but it was too late to back out now.

Maya looked over the notes she had jotted down and wished she had improved her public speaking skills. She normally was too shy to speak in public, but she realized she needed to make a concerted effort to improve if she wanted to affect the causes that mattered to her. For now, she needed to rely on the public speaking tips she had received from Jase, and the pep talk she had been given by Sister Lucy.

"Just think about what you can do to improve, instead of focusing on your fears. Figure out how you can be of service to others, how what you do can be dedicated to a higher purpose. You will find peace and meaning this way, and your words will reflect this," Sister Lucy had said when Maya told her she was going to meet her Congressman. It was the perfect piece of advice for Maya at this moment. She needed to set aside her own fears and focus on the bigger picture and what she was trying to accomplish.

Maya had written to her Congressman months ago. And when she hadn't heard anything, she had revised her letter and written to him again after conferring with Jase about it.

"Send another letter, Maya. Stay in front of them," Jase had advised her.

Recently, someone from the Congressman's office had responded. Maya had been so ecstatic when she received that letter, but equally disappointed that his office had asked for a donation in exchange for time with him, because he needed help with his upcoming re-election. They had implied it would be a small price to pay for time with the Congressman to hear their concerns.

She had tried calling Jeev weeks earlier, after he'd apologized for losing his cool with her. That was how he had referred to it when he called, "losing his cool." He seemed to have no memory of the physical injury he had given Maya, and he assumed she would forgive him. But Maya was in a bind, with no other connections in D.C. for help, and she needed to ask about the letter and the money, so she'd put aside her true feelings about Jeev and his lame apology and called him back. His only comment was, "I'm surprised you got a response, but don't bank too much on it. There's no way he could care about the issue you raised."

And when Maya had asked him about the donation the Congressman's office had requested, Jeev had laughed at her, loudly and for a prolonged amount of time.

"Maya, Maya, Maya. Don't you know by now, after everything I've told you, that's how it's done? Fundraising and lobbying. That's what moves Washington, D.C."

So Maya had acquiesced with the Congressman's office because apparently this was how things were done. She didn't know how to get around the request, and neither did her father's friends. Plus, she had heard enough times now that no Congressman ever entertained the invitation of a constituent in a private setting without some promise of something in return. So Maya had shared the letter with her father.

"Maya, I'm so proud of you. Look what happened after you persisted."

"But we will need to come up with the money," Maya said.

"What money?"

"I checked around. That's the way things are done. And I think there is a need to do something active to draw attention to the atrocities that have already taken place in Sri Lanka, despite the request by the Congressman's office for money."

So her father shared the letter with his friends, and the Swami family had agreed to host everyone. It turned out that while Maya was trying to get an audience with her Congressman, her father and the Swami family, as well as other families, had also been trying to get an audience with anyone who would listen. Everyone agreed that because this particular Congressman sat on the committee on foreign affairs, it was well worth a campaign donation to have the chance to speak with him.

At the Swami family's home, they shared the latest uncensored news from their direct contacts and short-wave radios about the ongoing events in Sri Lanka. Maya and her father shared their own harrowing experiences the past summer, describing the attacks and their suspicion that they'd been targeted, as well as their experiences in the refugee camp. They made sure to remind the Congressman that Sri Lanka is a part of the British Commonwealth, given that Britain was an important US ally. They shared the history of oppression and discrimination against the Tamil minorities, and the government pogroms over the decades, and more recently the possibility of genocide.

"The kidnappings of Tamil minorities, the raping of women in the minority community, the targeted killings have been continuing. Journalists are still being kidnapped as well, or more accurately, disappearing—but that has been going on for years, even before," Maya said to the Congressman.

The Congressman nodded, listening carefully.

Maya was unsure if his interest was sincere, but continued.

"Congressman, the government seems to be continuing to cover things up. The real news is being oppressed by the government sanctioned media outlets in Sri Lanka."

It was Maya's position, and that of her father and his friends, that the international public was being duped. That was why outside parties were not yet stepping up in larger numbers to mediate or help.

The Congressman continued to listen respectfully but asked no questions.

Maya told the Congressman, "In the past, no one has seemed to care about all of the oppression and discrimination and violence, and all of the humanitarian crimes. But it's time."

She defended the island country of Sri Lanka's importance in a few global economic areas, like tea and cinnamon and rubber and textiles. However, she knew it was hardly enough for the big countries to care. She knew the country had been marginalized for decades, and that it might continue to be marginalized if someone like the US did not step in. And even though the country was a part of the British Commonwealth, the British government seemed to have its hands tied, as well, for some reason or another.

"Well, I'm glad to be hearing your side of the story this evening," the Congressman said.

Maya took his comment as a small signal of interest and pleaded politely with the Congressman. "The American government is a chance at hope. Perhaps the US Congress could wield its influence in some way or take some action?"

The Congressman nodded noncommittally, and the evening ended with the Congressman drinking cocktails with everyone in the room, exchanging pleasantries, chuckling at guests' conversation as though unperturbed by all that he had just heard that evening, as if they had just been entertained by Scheherazade and her one thousand tales.

On the drive home, Maya said to her father, "I can't understand the casual response to everything we shared this evening. Do people have to actually experience the violence for themselves before they'll do something?"

Her father didn't answer.

#

Despite the disappointing end to their evening, the next day Maya felt elated that at last, someone with the power to help had listened to their story.

"Perhaps now there'll be some response from the American government. At least, I hope so," she said to her father. It was one of the rare occasions that they were home for dinner at the same time.

"I'm hoping that someone here might help to hold the government of Sri Lanka accountable," her father responded.

"And help extricate some of the people who are trapped there," Maya added.

Maya's father called his sister in Canada after dinner to tell her about the meeting with the Congressman, after Maya had retired to her bedroom. In their small house, Maya could hear him clearly from her bedroom.

"You must come down here and accompany me next time and share your story with the Congressman, too," her father said, sounding excited. "If there is a next time, of course. Maya's efforts came through, though, at least for now."

Then there was silence for several minutes.

Then she heard her father say, "Then I think it's time now that I also tell you about Vik."

Maya listened as her father filled his sister in on Vik's siding with the attackers, wondering how her aunt was taking the news.

"I don't know what happened either. I just don't know. I'm so sorry, Rosie," her father said. Her father listened, then said, "It's okay, Rosie. Don't cry. We made it out. We're here, safe."

More silence followed, then, "They just don't understand that here. The strife between Vik and his fellow Sinhalese brethren, versus the Tamil minorities. The people here, the government here, they don't comprehend the details, not yet. It's not a part of their daily news, and they don't know the history. So they need to be taught about what is going on. They need to be educated. That's what Maya was trying to do. That's what we were trying to do."

Maya wondered how interested the Congressman really had been to hear their story. There was so much going on in the world that the United States was involved in, particularly in the Middle East and the Soviet Union.

"Yes, yes," her father said. "I didn't forget about the stories from earlier years." Then Maya's father said goodbye to his sister and hung up.

When Maya and her father and brothers had originally left Sri Lanka in the early 1970s, they had wondered what had happened to her aunt Rosie who had stayed behind, whether she was okay. Later they would learn that Rosie had made it to Canada, but there were many years when her exact whereabouts and well-being were a mystery. Rosie had shared that in 1977, she had met up with her friends, which included a man named Vik, near Old Market in the northern part of the island, where there were large Tamil communities, to discuss Tamil poetry. Vik was not like her and her friends. He was Sinhalese, but he was interested in the writings of her Tamil community.

This friend Vik was the same man that her father had called out to during the attacks the past summer; the man who'd refused to help her father. Maya remembered what her aunt said had transpired after she reached her destination to meet her friends and Vik.

>"Thank God you did not leave," her aunt sighed, exhausted from her bike ride.
>"Of course we waited," Vik said.
>"Here, I brought an important book with me," her aunt said, taking a small, blue, tattered and uncovered hardback book from her purse.
>"Well, let's find somewhere to walk or sit," Vik said.

Then, Maya's aunt had told them, about fifteen minutes later, as they continued their discussions, lost in the buzz of the words, there had been a commotion in Old Market near the bus stand.

>Maya's aunt heard a cry.
>"This way, hurry!" Vik said, motioning violently with his right hand and parting the chaotic crowd with his left hand.
>The movement of the crowd was frenetic, panicked. Some people were shoved onto the ground, and Rosie and Vik quickly became separated from her friends.
>"Which way now?" Vik asked.
>"I don't know," she responded.
>Vik turned behind him to examine the dusty streets.
>"Quick, in there," a thin man said, motioning Rosie and Vik in the direction of what looked like a deserted bungalow.

Her aunt grasped at her frock and scuffled toward the bungalow. Brown dust kicked up by running feet clouded her eyes and nose. As they entered the moldy-smelling bungalow, Rosie tried to take in everything around her. What were they all going to do there? Where were they? Maya's aunt had become disoriented in all the harried running and turning.

Then shots rang out in the air.

"Quick, everybody duck underneath the table there," the thin man's voice said, and he pointed toward what looked like the kitchen.

Rosie grabbed the concrete wall for support as she took a step down into the sunken kitchen. She could see an old milk sanitizing machine in the corner, next to a deep basin sink. A wire cage sat next to the sink and the window above the sink looked out onto a small outhouse shed. In front of the sink was a large wooden table, and Rosie and Vik joined the others crouched underneath it. A car drove by with its radio blaring. Rosie could only make out a few words. "Police fighting... arrested..."

"What is going on?" Rosie wondered out loud, but her question was drowned out by the sound of a door slamming against a wall somewhere in the bungalow. She could barely make out the tired, huffing voice, sounding like it was coming from a small boy.

"There's fire in the streets and some shops... it looks like some people have been killed..."

Maya sat for a moment on her bed, thinking about Vik. She could not fathom how Vik had changed. How had he transformed from being friends with her aunt and interested in Tamil poetry to a person who wanted to violently persecute Tamils, including Rosie's own family? He had been her aunt's friend at one time, a friendship that transcended language and religion and culture. What had changed for Vik? Why was he part of a mob in the summer of 1983, attacking people he had once called friends?

#

Maya and her father and the others thought, after the evening at the Swami house, that the reception with the Congressman had gone well, but their confidence waned after weeks passed with no word from the Congressman's staff.

Finally, Maya got a letter from his office. She ripped it open in the foyer.

"What does it say?" her father called from the kitchen.

Maya read silently, tears welling up, her cheeks feeling hot. She sniffled a bit and looked up and tilted her head back, hoping her tears would not flow down her cheeks.

"Maya?" her father called out again.

Maya sniffled again and sighed. "Yes. The Congressman says he tried to speak to his fellow committee members. He says he tried to speak to members of Congress across party lines, and to anyone who was willing to listen to what he had learned from us."

Maya walked into the kitchen and joined her father at the table.

"Then what's wrong?" her father asked.

"He claims there were so many issues on the table in Congress that they needed to tend to, all of them urgent in some way or another, and that those issues were more urgent than what was going on in Sri Lanka," Maya said.

"I knew this would happen. This is what happens all the time. No one takes any of this seriously," her father said solemnly.

Maya took deep breaths while her aching chest felt as if it were plunging into her stomach. Once again, she felt unheard and unseen.

"*Calm down. Try not to be bothered by this. Think. What can you do next?*" a voice said in Maya's head.

It was the professor's voice, and she wondered why she hadn't called him, why she was procrastinating.

LIGHT

"I'll be fine, Jase. I've got this luncheon thing tomorrow with my family," Maya said. "And then we have that wedding Memorial Day weekend; that will be fun."

"I'm surprised your father was okay with me attending with you."

"Well, we haven't fully talked about the details. But he finally recognizes I'm an adult now, and we live in America, and that things are done a bit differently here. My mother was American, for goodness' sake."

Jase continued rubbing Maya's upper arms as he faced her. "Will you really be okay, though?"

"I think so. I'm trying, anyway. But can you promise you won't worry about me? I'll feel better if I know you're not worrying."

"But I am worried. You've been quiet ever since you heard back from the Congressman," Jase said. They were standing in the parking lot of their local gym and the sky was growing darker.

"I'm okay. I'm okay. Can we talk about something else? Can you tell me about your work? How are things going?"

Ignoring her question, Jase said, "Maya, I've been thinking. I think you need to tell me all of the details of what happened last summer. *All* of them. I think it's weighing you down and you don't even realize it. And it's like this big elephant in the room between us."

"I don't know…" Maya murmured softly.

"Well, can you at least tell me how you feel about all of it?"

"Guilty."

"Guilty? Why?"

"For surviving, maybe?" Maya said. "For feeling like I can't cope with not fitting in anywhere some days, even though I know I'm lucky to be here."

"Maya," Jase said, hugging her. "It's okay to feel however you feel. And I, for one, am very glad you survived."

"I'm not sure talking about it this much is a good idea. I don't want to burden you with all of this."

"It's not a burden. And look, I did some research," Jase said.

"You did research? About what?"

"I read about the problems in Sri Lanka over the past several decades. I can't say I understand what happened under British rule, but I do see that there were some really bad consequences. A lot of violence," Jase said. "And I just wish you'd tell me what happened to you."

"I told the Congressman we met with about it," Maya said. "Not the details, of course, but enough. And I just feel like nothing I'm doing is helping."

Jase nodded. "You've done a lot, Maya. You can't beat yourself up like this. You can't keep feeling guilty. You do have to live your life too, you know," Jase said, taking Maya's hand. "And by the way, I care a lot more about you than the Congressman does, you know."

Maya felt tears welling up. "I know," she said, squeezing Jase's hand and taking it up to her chest. "I'm so lucky to have re-connected with you."

#

Maya ran her fingers through her hair, her gold bangles, a gift from her grandmother, clanging on her arm as she combed each strand into place. She didn't like the feeling of the bangles on her arms but could imagine her grandmother's voice asking where the rest of her jewelry was.

"Where are your earrings? You're an adult now, of marriageable age. You need to look respectable, not disheveled."

The doorbell rang, announcing the arrival of the Swami family, followed closely by the Fernandes family. Maya could hear their voices down the hallway from her bedroom, her father greeting everyone cheerily as a new family, the Kerkovens, arrived.

Maya braced herself to join their guests. Mrs. Fernandes had been rude to her on several occasions now. Her daughter had not done well in college, and she seemed bothered that Maya had done well, as if the girls were in competition somehow. And Maya still did not feel that she knew the Swami family very well, since they never really talked much to her, only to her father. The Kerkovens were from Sri Lanka, too, but they looked a bit different from everyone else because they were from the Burgher community, a unique group that had been in Sri Lanka since the Dutch colonized the country. A few other families would join them, too; people her father knew from work.

Maya gave herself a pep talk, took a deep breath, and slid down the hallway with only hosiery covering her feet.

"Hi, Mrs. Fernandes," she said as she entered the family room, reaching with both arms to give the woman a quick hug.

Mrs. Fernandes had dark circles under her eyes. Her hair was pulled back in two plaits, parted down the middle, oiled as usual, and then pulled up in a bun, and she wore her usual minimal face cream and nothing else. Her macramé brown sweater clung tightly to her upper arms and upper chest, revealing a yellow, brown, and black colored sleeve underneath. Her tanned hands peeked out from the sleeves of her sweater, with thin fingers and even darker colored creases on the joints of her fingers.

"It was so nice of you to come today," Maya said, playing the part of dutiful hostess.

"When my daughter heard about this luncheon, she was jealous. She wished I had done this for her as she transitioned to adulthood," Mrs. Fernandes said. "Of course, we had to attend. If we were back home, I know more people would celebrate these types of auspicious occasions. But your father told me he struggled to obtain your agreement to hold this luncheon at all, which must be why it is a few months later than it should be."

Maya left the implied insult alone and excused herself from Mrs. Fernandes and headed to the kitchen to check on the food. She had helped prepare some of the dishes and wanted to be sure that everything that needed to be warmed was ready for the oven. As she bent to check that the oven was set on low heat, Maya overheard Mrs. Fernandes and Mrs. Swami speaking.

"Oh, those poor people," Mrs. Fernandes said.

"Yes, what more can we do, other than send them some money and hope it reaches the right people?" Mrs. Swami said in her raspy voice. "Oliver does too much."

"And Maya. Why do they try so much? Take it easy, that is what I say. Settle in and never look back."

"Maya is wasting her time," Mrs. Swami said.

"Those people back home are so poor, they'd be in a bad situation in any case," Mrs. Fernandes said. "And remember, there are people suffering on both sides."

"How do you mean, both sides?" Mrs. Swami said.

"You know the history."

"Of the persecution of the minorities, yes, I do," Mrs. Swami said, the volume of her voice rising noticeably.

"The Sinhalese people have also suffered under British rule," Mrs. Fernandes said.

"What suffering?"

"Come, now. You must remember. Lack of access to education and such."

"Those were decisions the British made," Mrs. Swami snapped. "That hardly justifies what the current government has been doing to the Tamil minorities."

Maya peeked out of the kitchen. The women were standing awkwardly next to one another, and Mrs. Fernandes was pressing the creases of her sari fabric with her fingers.

Mrs. Swami coughed and cleared her throat. "Anyway, Oliver told me that Maya has been quite active for a while now."

"But why waste so much time? Let the government help the people," Mrs. Fernandes said.

"That's precisely the problem. They're not helping. No one is," Mrs. Swami insisted. "And if there hadn't been so much persecution, there would still be Tamil communities there to help. But as it is, anyone who could leave, has left."

"Precisely. The cream of the crop has already gotten out. So what are the people left behind going to do?" Mrs. Fernandes said, cocking her head and crossing her arms.

"Everyone has potential, no? They should be helped. They can be educated," Mrs. Swami said.

"Hasn't that already been tried?"

"How is your daughter doing, anyway?" Mrs. Swami said, changing the subject.

"Oh, she's starting a new job already. The last one did not work out. She's nervous."

Maya made her way back to the family room.

#

On the Sunday of Memorial Day weekend, Maya and Jase headed to Uma's wedding in a suburb outside New York City. Uma was part of the Sri Lankan community, and several years older than Maya. Her family had moved to the US only a few years ago, which is when Maya and her father had reconnected with them.

Maya had always liked Uma, and felt sorry for Uma's mother, who had developed some mental health issues. She was very paranoid, always questioning other people's motives, and incapable of socializing with other parents. Uma basically had to raise herself, because her mother had cut off ties with most of their family friends, and it was only after Uma's mother died that Uma and her father were able to move to the US and try to repair those connections.

Maya had heard stories over the years about what Uma had endured and how toxic her mother's behavior had been towards her, and she suspected that Uma was still struggling. Having grown up without a mother, Maya understood the struggle of having no one to guide her, no one to help her adjust, no one to give her advice during the cruelest and most trying years of her life. But maybe Uma had it worse. She not only didn't have her mother's guidance, it sounded like her mother had actively worked against her. In trying to raise herself, Maya had made many mistakes, the kinds of mistakes that could have been prevented had someone been there to guide her, but she'd never experienced anything like what Uma had gone through with a mother who directly worked against her best interests.

Maya was lost in these thoughts as she and Jase drove the five hours to Uma's wedding. Her father had gone up a day early to reunite with some of his friends.

"You're quiet today," Jase said, glancing at her from the driver's seat. "Is anything wrong?"

"No. I was just thinking," Maya replied, stifling a yawn. She still couldn't sleep, still had nightmares, and still couldn't bring herself to tell Kelsie or Jase or Sister Lucy all that had happened.

And on top of being tired and anxious, Maya had realized that she was angry. Angry about what had happened in Sri Lanka, angry at Vik for participating in the violence, angry at Jeev for assaulting her, angry at Mrs. Fernandes for gossiping about her, angry at the Congressman's indifference, angry at herself for pretending to be fine rather than seeking help from a new therapist, or at least telling Jase the truth about what had happened.

Before she realized it, they had arrived in the parking lot of the wedding hall. It was empty, with only a dozen or so cars spread out in a parking lot that could hold over two hundred cars.

"Where is everyone?"

"I know. Strange, huh?" Jase said. "Or maybe Uma wanted a really small, intimate wedding. Some people do that nowadays."

They pulled into a shady spot under a tree and turned off the engine. Maya looked around the car to gather the wedding gift and her purse. She opened the door and grabbed her dress, a South Asian style sari, and lifted it up so that she would not trip on it getting out of the car. Only one more car had pulled into the lot.

Maya closed the door behind her and started walking toward the wedding hall with Jase.

As they entered the hall, Maya glanced at the priest and the few guests gathered for the ceremony, then took Jase's arm. They found seats on the bride's side, up in the front where Uma would see them and feel supported.

Maya picked up the wedding program. She glanced at it, then handed the program to Jase.

"It looks like it's going to be a long afternoon," he said, "plus the reception after the ceremony."

Guests began to trickle in slowly. Maya looked around the room. She did not recognize anyone. A group of women appeared at the back and lit something. They motioned with some metal plates and candles as a small group gathered.

143

Suddenly they were moving down the aisle toward the front, followed by a woman in a veil. Maya nudged Jase.

"That's her, I think. The bride."

The bridal party walked to the front and sat down. Uma joined the groom, who was waiting for her in the front of the wedding hall.

The ceremony was long, and at the end of it, Maya and Jase checked into the hotel where they were staying and went to their respective rooms to change clothes for the reception.

The reception was small, with even fewer attendees than the ceremony. Maya and Jase sat at the corner table talking to the other guests. One couple was from the same town where the groom was living and working, and another couple was there because they had previously worked with the groom. Maya was pleasantly surprised at how nice everyone was. She learned from them that the groom was a third generation American with family from Ireland. He had met Uma through friends at work and had been very vocal about the fact that he loved everything about Uma, including the many ways she was so different from him.

"Jase, look at how happy they are!" Maya said, as the newly married couple arrived and were introduced. "They have everything in front of them."

"I know. It's a nice thought. I wonder where they're going to settle down?"

Maya propped her elbows up on the table and clasped her hands in front of her. "You know Jase, seeing Uma has gotten me thinking."

"What are you thinking?" Jase said, grabbing the back of Maya's chair and pulling himself closer.

"That Congressman didn't come through for us. His committee couldn't come through for us."

"Yeah, and?"

"And Sister Lucy has been in contact with some charities that are on the ground doing humanitarian work."

"And?"

"It's still tough there for people. Dangerous. And my grandmother is still there. My father's relatives are still there."

"I don't know if I like where this is heading," Jase said.

"I know, I know. But—"

"Maya, it's not safe there. You're going to make me worry about you…"

"Would you worry about me?"

"Of course I would. Don't do it, Maya. It's not worth the risk. Stay here and do what you can from here."

"But I have to go back. Who else is going to help my family?" Maya whispered.

Jase examined her face, then let out a sigh of frustration. He looked down for what seemed like an eternity, then finally met her eyes. "I don't know if I can do this, then."

"What do you mean?" Maya asked.

"You and me," Jase responded.

"I don't understand," Maya said. "Just because I might travel back to Asia?"

"Maya, this is ridiculous. I want to help you and support you and do what I can, but you're talking about risking your life. Am I supposed to go along with that? Maybe I'm just being selfish, but I'd be lying if I pretended to be happy about this."

Maya sat silently. She had been so sure that going back was the only thing to do, but she also didn't want to lose Jase, and whatever it was that had developed between them.

Jase looked up and put his hand on Maya's hand. "I don't know how I'm going to cope with you being gone…much less the idea of you risking your life." He put his arms around Maya and pulled her closer to him, saying, "I can't make any promises if you go back."

#

A few weeks later, pushing through the uncertainty she felt about her plan and the emptiness of not having spoken to Jase since Uma's wedding, Maya visited Sister Lucy to say goodbye to her, and then went to Kelsie's house.

"How long will you be gone?" Kelsie asked.

"I don't know yet. Hopefully only a week or two, but I don't know," Maya said.

"Hopefully… I am worried about you."

"I'm not going to be alone. I'm going with my father. So don't worry, please."

"You've already done a lot, Maya."

"But not enough."

"You're too hard on yourself."

"Nothing has worked. And our family is there. So this seems like the best thing we can do."

Kelsie looked at Maya with sad eyes.

"I have to go. I need to go. I even told Jeev about it," Maya said.

"Jeev? You told Jeev you were going? Why?" Kelsie asked, recoiling in surprise.

"I don't know. I thought maybe there was something he could do to help."

Maya had surprised herself when she'd reached out to Jeev again. She couldn't explain why she hadn't just cut off ties with him after that terrible incident. He had nothing to offer. Not help, and not friendship.

"He always came across as someone who has ulterior motives," Kelsie said, surprising Maya.

"You thought that? Why didn't you tell me?" Maya asked.

"I don't know. I suppose I always wanted to give him the benefit of the doubt."

"Well, you're not too off on that."

"What do you mean?"

"He, umm, he assaulted me a few months ago. Physically."

"What?! Why didn't you tell me?!" Kelsie exclaimed, grabbing Maya's shoulders.

"I don't know. I think I was more shocked by the things he told me. Like that his father is connected with the so-called freedom fighting groups there."

"Why on earth did you tell Jeev you were going to Sri Lanka?" Kelsie said. "Why would you speak to him ever again after he was horrible to you?"

"I don't know. I can't explain it, Kels," Maya said. "Let's talk about something lighter, okay? What about you? What are you going to do this summer?" Maya asked.

Slowly, Kelsie broke out in a smile. "I'm going to Norway for a few weeks to visit relatives. I'm taking a break from work."

"That sounds really great," Maya said.

"It's more than that, though," Kelsie said. "There's an organization there that does some humanitarian work I'm interested in. I'm going to be visiting with them, too, to see what I can learn." Kelsie laughed lightly. "To tell you the truth, I'm really nervous and not fully sure what to expect."

"I can't wait to hear about it when you get back."

Maya left Kelsie's house feeling a strange sense of both liberation and apprehension. This was not the life she had imagined for herself, but it was both freeing and daunting at the same time. She was free to make her own choices, with no obligations or expectations holding her back, but she hadn't realized how difficult or lonely it would feel. She certainly hadn't expected to come face to face with her own mortality at such a young age, and she wasn't sure she was doing the right thing, but she had a nagging suspicion that she needed to resolve her past in order to move forward.

PART FOUR

*"Reject your sense of injury, and the
injury itself disappears."*
—Marcus Aurelius

THE WILL, THE SPIRIT

By June, Maya could no longer deny that she felt it imperative that she return to Sri Lanka. She could no longer sit idle. She had learned too much about how people can turn on one another through Jeev and Vik and the gossip of the women in her community, plus the impotence of the Congressmen and those she had tried to engage, their own inability to mobilize help here, and the discovery around how political influence works at the higher echelons of government. The world seemed like a cruel place, and the lives of people they knew and cared for—innocent people—were at stake, and no one else seemed to care. She needed to take action.

Maya's father was pacing in the kitchen, clearly agitated. They were scheduled to leave for Sri Lanka in just two weeks, but her father was suddenly having reservations.

"It's not going to be comfortable," he said.

"I realize that. I'm not looking forward to using that dingy outhouse again or all the lizards crawling on the walls while we sleep, but—"

"And it's no place for a woman right now."

"No place for a woman? Dad, come on."

"But regretfully, this is the reality of the situation there."

Maya sighed in frustration. "You know how I feel about this."

Maya's father shook his head slowly. "Okay. I know. You know we won't be staying in any decent places, though. We'll have to go all the way back to my old home… I'm not even sure what the state of the houses or the towns will be."

"I'm prepared for all of that."

"There may be wreckage from the fighting. I don't know what is still standing," Maya's father said. "I'm not even sure we will make it to my mother's home."

"Why wouldn't we? Because of the mobs?"

He nodded. "There may be army checkpoints, too. Or checkpoints by other groups. They may not allow people into certain areas," Maya's father said. "But there is a temporary quell in the fighting, so maybe not. But who knows how long that will last?"

"So, now is the time to go. It may be our last chance," Maya interjected.

"I know that. I feel the same way."

"I've tried everything I can think of here, but nothing has worked."

Maya's father relaxed and reached out to pat Maya's shoulder. "Yes. I know. I know I haven't said it, but I am proud of you for your effort."

"So this may be our only chance to do something."

Maya's father nodded. "Yes. I'm also going to take care of some other things while we are there."

"Like what?" Maya asked.

"Some legal issues related to land we still have there. And you need to know…" He stopped speaking abruptly and looked at Maya.

"What is it?"

"I don't know if any of our relatives will want to leave."

Maya nodded solemnly. "I know. I know you tried before. But

THE WILL, THE SPIRIT

now, after everything that's happened, we have to try again to get them out."

"Yes, it's worth trying. But your grandmother is old. She's unwell."

"I know. All the more reason why we need to go," Maya said.

"We will have to rely on guides to take us. It may be that we can only travel at night."

"How do you know all this?"

Without hesitation, her father said, "Swami uncle."

"What?"

"Swami uncle gets word from an NGO on the ground. Someone will be told of our arrival and will help us get through."

Maya was silent for a moment, digesting everything. It was all starting to sound more dangerous than she had initially thought.

"We'll have to go back to where grandmother is, back north to Jaffna, right?"

Her father nodded.

"Is that also where this land that you mentioned is located?"

He nodded again.

"And the fighting there has slowed down, but it's still going on?"

Maya's father let out a sigh. "Yes. Anything could happen."

Maya paused, internalizing once again the gravity of the risks she and her father would be taking.

Her father looked at her and started to speak, but Maya cut him off.

"I'm an adult. I'm still going. I'm not asking for permission. I'm telling you I'm going." Maya couldn't believe what was coming out of her mouth. She had never spoken this way with her father in the past.

"When did you become so outspoken like the Americans?" her father asked, taken aback. "Is this my daughter?"

Maya softened but held steadfast to her convictions. "Dad, sorry, but I need to go."

"You're sure you want to risk your life? You don't have to do this," Maya's father said.

"You don't have to either, do you?" Maya said, then immediately wanted to take the words back.

"Look…I didn't go back sooner because I had a duty to be here, for you and your brothers."

"I understand," she said. "But we'll be okay. I know you're worried because I'm a female, and I understand, I really do. But as you said, this may be the only chance, and I have to take it. We can take it together."

"Okay," Maya's father said, nodding. "I will call your brothers and tell them our plans." He reached out and touched her shoulder awkwardly, trying to show support. "I know you can handle yourself."

#

Maya's father searched frantically for their passports as they neared the first checkpoint in Sri Lanka. The long flight from the US to England to Sri Lanka, plus several hours of train travel from the capital city of Colombo in the South up to the North, had left them both completely exhausted. The train had stopped several hours away from their final destination and now Maya and her father would have to rely on a variety of paths and people to get to their final destination.

They were on foot and had been walking nearly twenty minutes in the tropical summer heat with the sun beating on them. The road was dusty and bumpy, full of stones that jutted into the soles of their shoes. Maya had already stopped several times to blow dust out her nostrils. She was so grateful they had packed light, only one bag each.

Her father fumbled with his shirt buttons as they got closer to the checkpoint, apparently undecided whether he should leave their passports in the thin document bag he had tied against his chest, or if he should take them out for the checkpoint soldiers.

He had already shaved off his short-lived Tamil-style mustache to blend in with the rest of the majority in the southern part of the country where they had arrived. In the North now, he thought they would be confronted by soldiers from the freedom fighting groups, but he wanted to be prepared in case there were soldiers from the government army.

"If my face doesn't give me away, the mustache may have. I don't know if I've compromised myself too much in this one simple act, Maya."

It was too late to think about all of that.

"ID please," a soldier said.

Maya's father produced two pieces of paper from his bags and quickly handed them over. The soldier examined the papers for several minutes, then he shuffled them and handed them back to Maya's father.

"You will have to go through another checkpoint if you want to enter this region. Walk about ten minutes and you will see it. Go to the man there, and he will perform the next inspection," the soldier said.

Just as they'd been told, about ten minutes ahead there was a dark-skinned man with dark hair and a mustache, dressed in a yellow-green uniform. The soldier allowed them to pass after inspecting their bags and their US passports.

"We need to walk for about twenty or thirty more minutes now," Maya's father said when they were away from the soldier. "Are you tired?"

"I can do it."

"We should come to the bus station then. We'll take a bus for about thirty minutes to the last stop."

"Is that the final destination?"

"No. Then we have to walk another thirty minutes to the lagoon."

"The lagoon? Won't it be dark by then?"

"Nearly, but we'll have to cross the lagoon. Then we walk to another bus. We will take that bus for about twenty minutes, then exit at the end of its route and walk again another ten minutes."

Maya was exhausted just listening, but she knew she needed to buck up and prepare.

#

It was the last hour of sunshine and there was no shade to be found as Maya and her father waited for the boat that would take them across the lagoon.

Maya's father pulled out the newspaper that he had bought back at the airport in London and plopped himself down on top of his duffel bag. Maya guessed he was looking at stock prices, since he'd expressed his concern several times recently that he hadn't saved enough for retirement.

Maya sniffed the air. She couldn't place the smell of the lagoon. Was it rotting grass? She pulled out her thin copy of George Orwell's *Animal Farm* and stood awkwardly with her satchel on her arm, reading a few pages at a time, picking up from where she had left off during their flight.

Their solitude was interrupted by a thin, tanned man with gray hair that was slicked back from his forehead.

"Oliver, is that you?" he nearly shouted.

"Do I know you?" her father replied.

"My gosh, Oliver! I have not seen you since our college days! At least twenty-five or thirty years," the man exclaimed.

Her father appeared to be struggling to place the man's face, trying to remember his name. "I'm sorry, forgive me. It has been too long for me. What is your name?"

"It's me, Jaya," the man said.

Her father paused, then his face lit up. "Jaya! The same fellow who graduated with such high honors that he won a fellowship to do research in England?"

Jaya exploded in a hacking chuckle, shielding his eyes from the sun. "Yes, that was me."

"Jaya, I have not seen you since our graduation! How I admired you. Did I hear you pursued an academic career?"

Jaya nodded. "I came back here to teach. I am on a break now, trying to head north to check on relatives."

Maya returned to her book as they continued to chat. Jaya looked so much older than her father, it was shocking to her that the two were apparently the same age.

The horizon transitioned to a purplish pinkish hue as the sun began to set. After reminiscing for several minutes, Jaya wandered off to find a place to sit down, and Maya's father returned to his newspaper. The air had begun to cool off, but it was still very hot.

Shortly after sunset, three men appeared with boats. They waited until the sun was down, then took out small flashlights and motioned to the people waiting to follow them onto the boats.

Nine or ten people began walking and boarded each of two boats, their feet, shoes, and shins getting wet from trudging through the water. Many were clutching their bags and personal belongings on top of their heads, and the atmosphere was still and heavy. Even the children stayed silent.

Some of the men remained in the water to push the boats away from the shore before climbing in. Maya could hear the water sloshing against the sides of the boats. She felt uncomfortable in her soaked clothing and shoes but remained still. Her father had stayed outside the boat to help the men push them away from the shore, and at the last minute he, too, climbed in, causing the boat to rock with his weight.

By the time they departed, there was little visibility, not even stars shining in the sky. It was difficult to make out the shapes of the other people on the boat. Maya could feel they were moving slowly and could hear the men who were rowing grunting in rhythm. She thought she could hear the other boat behind them, too, and the sound of the oars making rhythmic contact with the water. One man quietly explained that the boats ran the risk of being targeted or shot at during the daytime, and that was why they needed to row at night, when it was darker and quieter.

Time seemed to slide by in the darkness, until finally the boats began to slow. The man leading the boat indicated they would be stopping soon, near an embankment, and that they would once again have to trudge through the water to the shore.

Once the boats came to a stop, each passenger climbed out backwards, then reached back into the boat to grab their bags and personal belongings. Maya and her father again walked through the water clutching their belongings on top of their heads.

On the shore, another group of men greeted them and guided them through a thick forest. The smell of the trees and soil mixed with the odor of rotting grass that clung to Maya's clothing.

They were given flashlights, one per every two people, and were told to hold them facing down only, so as to draw the least amount of attention.

"What happened to the idea of walking to another bus?" Maya asked her father after they'd walked for nearly an hour.

"I don't know. It seems there is a ride arranged for us," her father replied. He told Maya they were walking a few miles to a pickup point.

After twenty or thirty minutes of walking, they arrived at a clearing in the forest and again waited for several minutes before a van pulled up to the clearing. They were instructed to board through the back opening of the van. No one said anything else. No one checked for any more documents. Maya could smell diesel gasoline, and her nostrils stung.

Inside the van, there were no seats, and as the van moved forward and swerved with each turn, everyone inside the back of the van moved in the direction opposite of the turn. Maya was caught each time by her father, who was holding on to a short square piece of metal jutting out from the right side of the van.

There was little conversation inside the van. Maya still could not make out any of the faces in the dark, and they had not seen Jaya, who had boarded the other boat and a different van, again.

After what seemed like over thirty minutes of driving through back roads in the pitch dark, they were dropped off on the road.

"We'll need to walk from here. I know the way. It's only about ten minutes," Maya's father said. "You must be tired?"

"It's ok. We are almost there now."

Maya had fully lost track of time at this point, and she was so far beyond exhaustion that it didn't seem worth mentioning. Walking behind her father in the dark, Maya nearly collided with him when he stopped abruptly in front of a wall. Behind the wall they could see the roof, just barely, of what appeared to be a bungalow. There weren't other homes nearby on either side, at least not that could be seen in the darkness.

"Why is it so dark?" Maya asked.

"I think the government is still not allowing electricity in this part of the North. There are no street lights yet," Maya's father responded.

They let their belongings hang more loosely around them, relieving their arms, and approached a gated entrance through the walls.

The walls were high enough that Maya, standing on the street, still couldn't see too much above them and still couldn't make out much other than a roof and the tops of some windows with iron rods across them. As she approached the bungalow, she could see the walls were of the fading yellowish brownish concrete.

"This is it," her father whispered, reaching for the latch on the gate.

"This is what?" Maya responded, clutching her satchel, tired from the endless journey and all the transitions.

"Your grandmother's house. Don't you recognize it? She is likely sleeping."

They walked through the gate and her father closed the latch behind them. Maya followed him down a dirt path, past the front of the house and to the right, down the side, where they entered a dirt courtyard in the back and Maya saw an elevated back porch. The doors and windows were shut.

Her father walked up a pair of concrete stairs and tried turning the door handle. It didn't budge, so he moved to the window adjacent to the door and put his face up to it. Then he walked the length of the back porch looking through each window. Dissatisfied, he returned and knocked on the door, simultaneously placing his ear against the door and announcing in a loud whisper that it was him, that her son had returned.

A young man opened the door and looked at her father momentarily and then hugged him. Maya didn't recognize the young man, but he showed them a place to the side of a dining room where they could sleep. The young man explained no one used that room, and then he pointed to rolled up mats leaning against the dining room wall.

It was dark and hot, and Maya was feeling extremely sweaty, but she placed her belongings on the dining room table and unraveled the woven flat mat and spread it out across an open space on the floor. Her father did the same on the opposite side of the room. Maya laid down to sleep with her arm across her forehead, exhausted after all the demanding travel and logistical shifts they had completed in the past twenty-four hours.

#

Maya woke to the sound of a dog barking out in the courtyard and the smell of curry leaf and orange pekoe tea wafting through the air. She opened her eyes and looked up at the ceiling and the beetles and flies circling above her. The floor felt very hard beneath her back. Maya got up and rolled up her mat and leaned it again against the wall near the dining table.

She pulled out some fresh clothing from her satchel and quickly changed her clothes, then walked out to the back porch and was greeted by Jack, her grandmother's dog, and the source of all the barking. Her father was at the other end of the porch sitting on a chair next to his mother, Esther. She looked different than Maya remembered. She was grayer, more hunched over, more tired in her eyes. Amazing the toll one horrible year could take on a person.

Maya's father turned to her. "Come, Maya. Say hello to your grandmother. And have some of these. I just sliced them fresh now. It's mango season."

Maya's mouth started watering, looking at the sliced mangoes on the plate her grandmother held. She smiled at her grandmother and picked up a piece of mango and took a seat on the bench next to the old woman. She was instantly flooded with the smells of her grandmother's leathery skin and the cotton and polyester of her clothing simmering in the heat.

Her grandmother did not hug Maya, but rather said in her mixed Sri Lankan and British accent, "Now we must get you a proper cup of tea. But first, tell me, what have you been doing this past year?"

Maya opened her mouth to speak but her grandmother interrupted.

"Don't tell me in English, Maya."

Maya started again slowly, in halting Tamil, her birth language. It was the same language that her grandmother Esther had painstakingly learned after she had settled on the island. Maya spoke in broken sentences, trying to explain how the year had gone, finishing up college, applying for jobs and graduate school, college for the twins, who had stayed behind in the US because of their summer job internships. She found it difficult to speak fluently and was shocked by how much she had forgotten.

Her grandmother looked down and nodded, listening to Maya. At the end she patted Maya on the shoulder, saying, "You must keep up your language skills. You mustn't forget."

Maya nodded, feeling somewhat disappointed at the emotionless interaction between her and her grandmother, and rose saying she would go play with the dog in the courtyard.

"Jack is his name, remember, short for Jackfruit," her grandmother said.

Maya started to say that she knew this already, then decided against it.

"Maybe I'll take him for a short walk in front of the house and then come back," Maya said. As she turned the corner of her grandmother's front yard, she noticed that her grandmother's beloved hibiscus flowers were missing, and her garden bed was disheveled. It had been destroyed.

The dining room where Maya slept faced the street, and when she stood on one of the chairs, she could see out the tops of the windows. Mostly the streets were empty, but from time to time she would see people sauntering by in the mornings and evenings, probably trying to keep as much a sense of normalcy as possible with a daily walk. On several occasions she noticed a white van pass by the house in the evenings. It was the same white van every time because it always had its windows rolled down and blared the same song each time it passed by.

One evening the white van stopped in front of the walls of her grandmother's bungalow and two men dressed in tattered cargo pants and plain t-shirts emerged. Maya could see them walk through the front gate and she soon heard deep voices asking to speak with the man of the house.

Maya could hear her father's voice answering. There was something aggressive in the men's voices and she remained in the dining room listening.

The men were telling her father about various rebuild projects in town.

"We insist you come and see the projects," one of the men said.

Her father tried to placate the men. "Okay, okay, machan, another time then. Maybe another day I'll come and see. I'm only here now to check on my mother."

Maya could hear him walking and talking with the men as they exited through the gate in the front of the house. Finally, she heard the van revving off in the distance.

When Maya's father returned to the back porch, she asked him what the men had wanted.

"I'm not one hundred percent sure," her father said, "but I think they may be local men who are trying to collect money to complete their rebuild projects."

"Are they with one of those groups? The freedom fighters?" Maya asked.

"Do you have to go with them, Oliver?" her grandmother asked as she joined them on the porch.

"I think so, eventually."

"Why would you go with them?" Maya asked.

"Before we left, Swami uncle told me he had heard about groups like this," her father said. "They approach people from out of town to ask for money, maybe. I'm not quite sure," her father explained.

"And do you have to go just because they ask?" Maya said.

Maya's father shrugged. "I don't know."

"Are we under watch now?" Maya asked, beginning to feel an uncomfortable churning in her stomach.

"They obviously know we are here. If they come back, I may have to do what they say." He was quiet for a minute, then said, "I haven't quite figured out yet who these groups are. These may be clandestine groups, operating under the threat of retribution from the government. I may have to go along with them until I figure it out."

"I'm just an old granny, so they haven't been bothering me here," Maya's grandmother said.

#

The next morning, Maya heard commotion outside the dining room window. She stood on a chair to look outside and her stomach turned somersaults at the sight of the white van. As she climbed down from the chair, she nearly fell, and had to sit on the floor to catch her breath. There was a loud yell from the gate, and then Maya heard her father's voice. It sounded like he was pleading, reasoning with the men. She heard the sound of a car door closing, then the roar of the engine as the van sped away.

Maya walked out to the back porch to look for her father, but he wasn't there. She went back inside the house and walked down the corridor, looking into each room as she passed. She did not see her father, or her grandmother, or even the young boy who helped her grandmother around the house.

Maya went into the kitchen. Her grandmother was leaning with both hands on the kitchen sink, looking down.

"Grandmother?"

Her grandmother groaned.

"He's gone, isn't he?" Maya asked.

"I couldn't do anything," her grandmother said, shaking her head. "I'm just an old lady."

#

Maya's sense of dread grew with each hour that her father failed to return to the house. She tried to distract herself with her book and the dog, but finally gave up and went searching for her grandmother. She found her sitting on a bench in the corridor.

"He's been gone a long time," Maya said. "More than twelve hours."

"I know," her grandmother said, her two hands gripping the cane she was leaning onto.

"And it's been dark for hours. What could they be doing?"

"In Tamil, child. Speak Tamil."

Maya repeated the same question to her grandmother in Tamil.

"I don't know," her grandmother responded in Tamil.

Thoughts were swirling in Maya's head, but she stuffed them down and grasped for something else to talk about.

"I didn't know you used a cane," Maya said.

"Only sometimes," she responded in English. "It was so dark. I didn't want to fall walking over here."

"He's been gone for too long," Maya said. "I'm worried. We need to do something."

"I'm just an old lady. What can I do?"

"Is there anyone here I can call?" Maya asked.

The nearest neighbors were over one mile away, the old lady said, but she didn't know them. "And I don't have a telephone here."

"How do you get in touch with people then?"

"Usually by letter."

"What if there is an emergency?"

"There is a telephone in the postal office."

"But how do you communicate with people? Other than by letter?"

"I wait for people to come by, to visit, and bring me their news." Esther sighed. "Of course, when I was younger, I would walk several miles into town every few days."

"Okay, so let's say I go to the post office and ask to use their telephone. Who could I contact that could help us? Should I call the police?"

"I don't know if we can trust the police."

#

The next morning, after having abandoned the conversation with her grandmother that was going nowhere, and trying and failing to sleep, Maya rose from the mat on the floor. She rolled up the mat and leaned it against the corner of the dining room. The house was quiet, which meant her father still had not returned.

Maya tried to swallow the lump of dread in her throat and went to find her grandmother in the kitchen.

"I'm going to polish the dining room floor," Maya said after they'd exchanged greetings. "It will give me something to do while I think. Then I will draw water from the well and take a bath."

"Over there," her grandmother said, pointing her chin toward the corner of the kitchen.

"What's that?" Maya asked.

"You'll need coconut scrapings for the floor. Scrape some coconut with the serrated blade, then take the scrapings and put it on two sponges," her grandmother said. "Use it to polish the floor."

"With my hands?"

"With your hands if you want to crouch down. Or with your feet if you want to stand up. Remember to slightly wet the sponges first so the coconut sticks to it."

Maya scraped some coconut in the kitchen and then found two sponges from her grandmother's kitchen and carried them all together back to the dining room. She sprinkled the coconut scrapings on the sponges and then bent down to start polishing. She was astonished at how well the coconut oil from the scrapings on the sponges were polishing the floor, and the repetitive work helped take her mind off of the panic she felt about her missing father as she weighed her options.

When her back began to ache, Maya stood up and stood on the sponges instead, one foot on each, and began skating across the floor on top of the sponges. Once she was satisfied with how the floor looked, she returned the sponges to the kitchen and went out to the back porch and started pacing. It was nearly midday and her father still had not returned.

As Maya paced, she realized she would not be able to replicate or retrace her steps, as so much of the travel between the train station and this location had been done through unmapped paths and unofficial transportation vehicles, much of it in the dark. She didn't even know how to get back to the train station, much less the airport. She would have to go to the post office and try to make an international call, maybe to Swami uncle, or better yet, the US embassy. Surely they would help.

Maya walked back inside and found her grandmother on the bench in the corridor again.

"It's past midday and he hasn't returned," Maya said.

"Yes," was all her grandmother said.

"Do we need to come to terms with the fact that appa might have been kidnapped?" Maya asked, trying not to sound as panicked as she felt.

"I'm not sure," her grandmother responded, staring straight ahead.

"Have you heard about this happening to anyone else?"

"I've heard rumors," her grandmother said, turning to look at Maya. "But you know how rumors are. They are difficult to confirm. And people are too afraid to speak about it."

"What about the embassy?" Maya asked. "Maybe they can do something to help. I need to call them."

"How will you contact them?" her grandmother asked.

"Can I walk to the post office from here?" Maya asked, struggling to keep the frustration out of her voice.

"You can, but it is a far walk," her grandmother replied. "Three miles."

"Then I should go now."

Maya pulled on her sandals and asked her grandmother if she could take Jack with her. When her grandmother nodded and handed her the dog's makeshift leash, Maya set out on the dusty road for the post office.

When they got to the post office, Maya asked the man at the counter to help her place a call, and if he knew how to contact the US embassy. Using the rotary phone, he accepted her request and tried asking the operator to transfer them to several contacts Maya knew of through her father and her own research back in the US, but they got no answer at all, not even for the embassy. Blinking back hot tears of frustration, Maya took Jack's leash in her hand and left.

#

On the morning of the third day after her father's disappearance, the white van pulled up in front of the wall in front of the bungalow. Maya knew it immediately because she recognized the song blaring from its windows. She stood on the chair to look out the window. The van was idling in front of the house, but no one got out. The windows of the van were dark, and after a few minutes, the van pulled away.

Maya walked quickly back to the corridor where her grandmother was in her usual spot on the bench. Jack was standing next to her grandmother, his fur sticking straight up, snarling and barking.

"Something has gotten in the house, I suspect," Maya's grandmother said.

Maya shushed the dog and walked down the corridor, poking her head into each of the rooms. When she saw her father lying on one of the beds, she let out a scream.

Her grandmother turned her neck sharply and pushed herself off the bench. "What is it?" she said.

"He's here!"

"What? Oliver?"

Maya ran to her father, who held up his hand, asking them to stay back. Maya nodded and went back into the corridor.

"He's getting up," she said.

Several minutes later, Maya's father appeared wearing the same clothing he had been wearing three days earlier.

"Where were you?" Maya said, tears flowing down her cheeks. "We thought you had been kidnapped."

Her father took a seat on the bench. "I'm okay."

"What happened?" Maya asked. "Why were you gone so long?"

Her father exhaled audibly, then said, "They showed me all their projects in this area."

"What? Why did it take so long? When did you get back?" Maya asked.

"Very late last night. Or rather, this morning. I didn't want to wake you," her father replied.

"Why did they keep you so long?"

"I don't know. They asked me for money to fund their projects, over and over again. I told them I had no money, but they kept insisting."

"And?" Maya asked, her eyes widening.

"They didn't harm you, did they?" her grandmother asked.

Maya's father shook his head.

"Do you know who they were?" Maya asked.

"I'm still not sure," her father responded, scratching his chin.

"Did they say their names at any point?" Maya asked.

Her father was silent for several minutes, his eyes closed as if he were thinking. "They mentioned someone by the last name of Raja," he said finally. "Raja from the US."

"The US? Are you sure?" Maya asked, nausea rising in her throat.

"What is going on, Maya?" her grandmother asked.

"Did they say anything else?" Maya asked.

"They were frustrated, I think. Raja was meant to send money to help them. That's the impression I got. But it wasn't working out the way they wanted."

"I think I know who they were referring to," Maya said, beginning to pace.

"Maya, what are you talking about?" her father asked. "Calm down."

"I should have listened to my instincts about Jeev. I should never have told him we were coming."

"Who is Jeev?" her father asked.

"From my old school. He works at a law firm in Washington, D.C. I contacted him when I thought he could help."

"I don't understand?"

"His last name is Raja. His father has connections in Washington. Jeev told me his father also was connected with groups that are fighting the government here. They must have thought you would help fund their activities."

They were all silent for a long time.

Finally, Maya's grandmother spoke. "What did you see?" she asked. "When they took you around, what did you see?"

Maya's father let out a sigh. "Each day they drove me somewhere different. Areas they have begun to rebuild. Places that had been destroyed by attacks or gunfire or fires over the years." He paused for a minute. "I do know there are some legitimate organizations in the US and Canada that are assisting with rebuilds and such. Swami uncle and I have discussed it. I don't know who these men are aligned with, but obviously, their tactics are improper, to say the least."

"I think we need to leave soon," Maya said, sitting down next to her grandmother.

"I think you are right," her father said, then he turned to his mother.

"You need to come to the US. You and the boy."

Her grandmother sighed. "I'm too old now. My place is here. This is my home."

"You've said that before. But surely you don't think you're safe now?" Maya asked, her voice rising in frustration.

"Normally no one comes around here," her grandmother said. "Maybe it's because I'm English. And I think the boy is safe with me."

The argument with her grandmother continued for several days, but the old woman never wavered. She was determined to stay in her home for as long as she had left to live, and she was certain that her Britishness would keep both herself and the boy who lived with her safe from harm.

Maya used her remaining days to try to make contact with some of the dioceses in Sri Lanka that Sister Lucy had suggested, as well as some of the NGOs on the ground. She learned that in both cases, these organizations could only attend to civilians. They could not do anything to persuade the government to take accountability for what they had done.

Maya made a second and third walk to the post office, this time armed with the corrected contact for the US embassy that her father provided. She tried to learn what help was available for the other innocent people that were stuck here, and whether there were any refugee programs that could possibly help her father's relatives. The information she collected was not particularly helpful. It would not be easy for anyone to gain entry to the US on a work visa, and there were no established refugee programs there for this particular part of the world at this time. Filing for asylum would be a complicated and lengthy process.

\#

"At least move to one of the safer areas," her father pleaded with her grandmother a few days later.

"I will go if I have to, but not until then," her grandmother responded.

Maya could see that her father was angry with his mother for her stubborn attachment to this home, despite a grudging admiration for her loyalty to her adopted homeland.

"I hope you will respect that I can no longer remain here. I have an obligation to my children and to my employer," he said to his mother. "Maya and I will take leave tomorrow."

The old lady simply nodded.

\#

As they made their connection through London Heathrow on their way back to the US, Maya's father wondered out loud when he would next receive any contact from her grandmother. The communication lines had deteriorated markedly between the North and the remainder of Sri Lanka, much less the rest of the world, and Maya suddenly realized just how much worry her grandmother was placing on him by refusing to leave. If she'd agreed to come to the US, her father wouldn't have to spend every waking moment wondering if his own mother was still alive.

As she arranged herself in her seat for the last leg of their trip, Maya felt unsettled by the visit. Going back to Sri Lanka hadn't resolved anything. All she had learned is that it would be nearly impossible to get any relatives or others out, and there were numerous groups battling within Sri Lanka who did not see eye to eye with each other and were willing to let politics take precedence over concern for innocent lives. What had they accomplished?

Maya felt a veil of gloom descend upon her. She wondered how she would move forward.

HEAVY

The night sweats and nightmares returned as soon as Maya got home. Her anxiety was at an all-time high, and she often could not get out of bed. And to top it all off, she hadn't seen or spoken to Jase. He had gone silent on her, which only added to her anxiety.

Somehow she conjured up the energy to pack her bags and get dressed early in the morning on the day she had to report to her new graduate school at Duquesne. Maya had committed to teaching in the second half of a summer program there earlier that year, after she had been accepted into graduate school for her Masters in English. It would be her first real teaching job.

Maya knew she needed to put everything else behind her now and focus on her work and school. She did her best to seem cheerful as her father drove her to campus.

"I'm proud of you, you know," he said as they drove into campus. Maya had to fight back tears.

The campus was frenzied as a new batch of students arrived for a summer semester. Cars were double-parked and people were loading their personal items into rolling bins as quickly as possible. Maya walked up and down the student pathways near her assigned graduate student building to find a table for check-in. Once that was done, she got a rolling cart and took her belongings to her room, having said a quick goodbye to her father as soon as the car was emptied.

She placed her suitcases and other sundry items on the floor and brought her backpack to the desk in the tiny studio and began to unpack the few pens and notebooks she had brought from home. She had a list of errands to run—to the bookstore, to find a new typewriter, and there was a mandatory teacher preparation meeting the following day. She scanned the information on the desk about the library and looked at the campus map and stuck the magnet with crisis hotline numbers on it onto the tiny refrigerator in the corner.

"Hey, we're walking a few blocks to grab some food. Do you want to come?" a couple of other grad students said, stopping in Maya's open door. She was starting to answer when Kelsie poked her head in the door. Kelsie had promised to come and make Maya's first evening on campus a good one, plus Maya was dying to hear all about Kelsie's trip to Scandinavia.

The two of them joined the other graduate students to go out for an early dinner. They walked to a nearby diner and piled into a large booth, ordering chicken wings and french fries and pierogies to share. Maya watched as Kelsie chatted with the group, at ease among people she'd only met a few minutes earlier.

"So Maya, where are you from? Are you Persian?" one of the men asked.

"I'm part Asian, part American," Maya replied. "Born in the British Commonwealth," she added.

"That's cool. It's cool to have someone different in our group," the man said, nodding and chewing on a pierogi.

"Different how?" Maya asked.

"Oh sorry, I didn't mean that offensively," he said.

"Yeah, very cool," the woman next to Kelsie said. She laughed lightly. "I have an aunt who refuses to get to know anyone who isn't a direct descendant of someone on the Mayflower… I mean can you believe how snobby that is?"

"When you said you were born in the British Commonwealth, did you mean a former British colony?" the man asked.

Maya nodded.

"What's that like?" he asked.

Maya considered how she might explain the paradox that colonialism was for someone like her. As a minority in the country in which she was born, the monarchy and colonial leaders had been a source of stability at times, but on the other hand, perhaps colonialism itself had only underscored the inequalities that existed and created issues that hadn't existed before. And how could any country think it was okay to invade foreign countries and subjugate its people?

"Oh, that's a great topic for another day," she said finally. "It's a complicated answer."

After dinner, Maya and Kelsie walked back with the others and said their goodbyes, then went to Maya's room to chat.

"How was your trip to Norway, Kelsie?"

"It was so great! I don't even know how to explain it to you. I loved seeing my grandparents again, and the humanitarian organization was incredible."

"Yeah?"

"I think I might apply for a position there. I can really see myself there, if I can get an offer from them, that is. I feel like I'd be doing something, you know, meaningful."

"That's so fantastic! I remember you said you weren't happy with your other job. You sound so happy now."

"How about you?" Kelsie asked. "Did your grandmother come back with you? Or anyone else?"

Maya let out a whimper. "It's going to be harder than I thought. I feel so naive, Kels. I had no idea how hard it would be to help," she said, shaking her head.

"I'm so sorry," Kelsie said, placing her hand on Maya's

shoulder and pulling her in for a brief hug. "I know you're disappointed. Have you talked to Jase?"

Maya's cheeks flushed. "No, I haven't talked to him in weeks. He actually went silent on me," she lamented looking down. "I think he might be in Texas now for work and I'm not even sure when he's coming back."

Maya groaned softly and put her face down into her hands.

Kelsie was quiet for a few minutes. Finally she asked, "Have you talked to anyone about this? Please don't be offended, but you just don't seem like yourself anymore."

Maya could feel tears welling up inside. "My father went missing for three days in Sri Lanka," she said, looking up. "I thought he had been kidnapped."

"What? That must have been so scary!"

"It was. I'm just feeling kind of…lost, I guess," Maya said. "And I know I need to get myself together and focus on teaching."

Kelsie nodded, rubbing Maya's arm.

Maya let out a sigh.

#

Thanks to the demands of teaching, the weeks flew by and before she knew it, Maya's work for the summer session program was coming to an end. All that was left was to administer a final exam and collect the students' final submissions of work and she would be done. She was relieved the summer session was ending, but as students began to leave and the campus emptied out, Maya began to feel sad again. All of the thoughts she'd been able to avoid by staying busy came creeping back, and she missed Jase more than she wanted to admit. She missed the warmth of his breath when he spoke to her, the strength in his arms and shoulders when they locked elbows on their walks.

She missed having him to confide in. She wondered how things would have been different for her if her mother had lived, if she could have confided in her and gotten advice about Jase.

Maya knew she hadn't had time to process what had happened with their trip back to Sri Lanka, her father's kidnapping, and how impossible it seemed to help innocent civilians escape the country. She also recognized she had never fully processed Jeev's betrayal and assault on her, or the violent attacks and attempt at rape from which she had escaped the prior summer. She had never processed the fear she felt when she ran, the insecurity she felt as they awaited their uncertain future in the refugee camp, and the emptiness she had been feeling because she no longer could trust so many people. She had been searching for certainty and direction for ages, it seemed, and was always failing to find it.

She lay for an hour on her bed, her head propped on her hands and her legs and ankles waving in the air as she used to do when she was younger. It was comforting to revert back to that position. She thought about all the different people she had spoken to when she volunteered at the peer counseling group and hotline with Sister Lucy. So many of those people had seemed to be stuck in the same way Maya was, sad or frustrated or both. Many had hinted at doing something drastic to themselves, but Maya never wanted to assume anything for them, and always tried to talk to them and keep them on the line.

Maya decided to take a walk, maybe visit the drug store and get some sleeping pills so she could get a good night's rest for once. The thought crossed her mind that for many of the people she'd spoken to at the hotline, sleeping pills offered a means to an end, but she tried to push those thoughts away, and grabbed her books off her desk in her room and stuffed them inside her satchel. As she prepared to leave her room, she saw the magnet with the crisis hotline numbers on it again, and it dawned on her that one of the numbers was the same hotline where she'd volunteered. How had she missed that when she'd stuck the magnet up in the first place?

She grabbed the magnet and headed to the communal phone booth down the hall and dialed the crisis hotline number. After a few rings, someone picked up.

The voice on the other end was warm and familiar. It was Sister Lucy.

Maya began speaking. "I…I don't know why I called."

"That's okay, hon. Take it slow," Sister Lucy said.

Maya was relieved that Sister Lucy didn't seem to recognize her voice.

"I…" Maya couldn't think of what to say. She felt ashamed for feeling the way she felt. She felt ashamed for not having figured things out already. She felt the weight of her past on her, but also tremendous guilt for being sad when so many people were in real danger and had horrible problems to deal with. Her problems now were nothing compared to living in fear for your own life, but yet, she still couldn't seem to shake them.

"Go on, dear," Sister Lucy said.

"You don't know what it feels like to not know if there is anyone out there that cares about you," Maya blurted. "To know that you don't fit in anywhere, and to feel that pain over and over again."

"Take it slow, dear. Tell me what you mean."

Maya was silent for a moment while she collected her thoughts. "To have your own government betray you," she said finally. "It's just…there's no one to trust."

"Government? Where are you from, dear?" Sister Lucy asked.

Maya hesitated. "I wasn't born here, but now I'm American," she said finally.

"Go on."

"Well, it's just, it feels awful to have everyone around you stabbing you in the back." Maya started sobbing silently.

"What happened? Do you want to talk about it?"

"I just feel tired… I don't want to think about this anymore." Maya felt a sharp pang in her stomach, and she was beginning to regret that she'd called.

"Tell me how you are feeling, besides tired," Sister Lucy prompted.

"My chest really feels sore. It aches. My face feels congested. My head is pulsating."

"How long have you been feeling this way?"

"I don't know. Months, I guess."

"Well, I can say you are not alone. There are others who have felt this same way. And I'm glad you called me. May I ask where you are located?"

Maya didn't want to give away where she was, so she only mentioned she was in the greater Pittsburgh area.

"Ok," Sister Lucy said. "I want to give you the name of a doctor you can see in the area, whom you can talk to more regularly, and share your feelings. How does that sound?"

"I don't know. I'm not sure that would help."

"Well, I'll tell you what. I'll just give you the phone number, and you write it down. You can decide later whether you want to use it or not."

"I guess so."

"Or you can call us back, here, anytime."

"Alright. But I have to go get a pen and paper."

"I'll wait right here while you go get one, but promise me you'll come right back," Sister Lucy said.

"Okay, hold on." Maya ran to her room and returned with a pen and paper, relieved that no one else had come to the phone booth and hung up the phone receiver. "I'm back."

Sister Lucy gave Maya two numbers of a therapist and a doctor.

"Okay, I wrote them down."

"Do you have anyone else you can talk to? Maybe a parent or a trusted friend?"

"I really haven't had anyone to talk to, not like this…" Maya's voice trailed off.

"You haven't tried to hurt yourself at any point, have you?" Sister Lucy asked. "There's nothing to be ashamed of, you know. You can tell me anything."

"I might have drunk a bit much at times, thinking it might numb some of the thoughts in my head," Maya said, then stopped, startled by the sudden insight into her own past actions.

"That's okay," Sister Lucy said. "I want you to talk to those people I recommended. Can you promise me you'll do that?"

Maya said she would, then hung up the phone, overcome with both embarrassment and relief. Her chest was throbbing. Her face ached with the congestion after crying and her body felt limp and wrung out. She returned to her studio in a daze and peeled off her shoes then sat down slowly on her bed. *Why hadn't she just gone and bought the pills?* she chastised herself.

MONK

A few hours later, Maya's head was still spinning. Something subconscious warned her she shouldn't be alone right now. She needed to go out for a walk and be around other people, even strangers.

Outside, the air was cool, and Maya went for a walk, but soon found herself back at her room, too tired to go further. She kicked off her shoes again and lay down on the bed, hoping sleep would come quickly. Before she drifted off, she made a promise to herself. She wouldn't call the therapists Sister Lucy had recommended, but she would call the professor Sister Lucy had introduced her to years earlier.

#

Maya rose the next day, feeling hopeful for the first time in ages. She walked back to the communal phone booth, picked up the receiver, and dialed the only person she thought could guide her out of her mess.

When the professor answered, Maya reintroduced herself, but he interrupted, as if he'd been expecting her to call.

"Yes, yes, Maya, hello. What can I do for you?"

At first Maya was silent, trying to gather her words. Then she spoke slowly. "I have been distressed about something… Professor, so much has happened, and I couldn't think of anyone else who might understand."

"Tell me, Maya."

And so she did. She told him everything. About the feeling she'd always had of being an outsider, a foreigner who was perpetually out of step with her peers. How she'd missed her mother growing up, and sometimes resented her father for his preoccupation with the minutiae of his homeland. She told him about the attack the summer before, the nightmares in which she saw, over and over again, the burning housemaid, and felt the terror of watching the man unbuckle his belt. She told him about trusting Jeev and how he'd assaulted her, and how she suspected he'd set her father up to be kidnapped. And she even told him about losing Jase, and how punishing that felt when the trip back to Asia had been a huge waste of time and money, since they hadn't managed to help anyone, much less resolve Maya's angst. She told him how frustrated she felt about the world's indifference towards the atrocities in Sri Lanka, and how that only compounded her own feelings about being unseen and unheard in the world.

"Good, Maya. Good," the professor said when she'd exhausted herself. "You are questioning what you see in the world because you are starting to act based on reason. Most people act based on impulses. They don't take the time to think and question."

"So hatred and discrimination are just impulses?"

"Yes," the professor said. "They're certainly not rational. What reasoning could make someone hate another human being based simply on their skin color or language?"

"And the killings and rapes and kidnappings? All the violence—those are just irrational impulses, too?"

"Violence is often fear-based. People feel threatened and lash out. It's complicated, of course," he said. "But you're speaking of Sri Lanka, where long-standing resentments have festered, and now innocent people are paying the price."

"Thousands of people have been killed, and tens of thousands have been displaced," Maya said. "And I don't know what to do about any of it."

The monk cleared his throat. "You must focus on taking your energy away from negative things and move toward more positive things, such as the effort you will make to help in whatever way you think is right for you. Don't try to change others. Focus on changing yourself first. Focus on changing your perspective, your reactions, your actions."

"Okay…" Maya said, trying to take in everything he was saying.

"Focus on what you are thinking, on the thoughts you allow inside your head. You must put realistic positive thoughts inside your head. Your life becomes what you think, Maya," the professor said, sounding more like the monk he used to be than an academic.

"My life becomes what I think," Maya repeated.

"Yes. That is why you must be careful what you think, because it ultimately influences your actions."

"I understand, I guess."

"Remember, don't expect others to behave in the way you want them to behave," the monk continued. "You need to use knowledge, reflection, effort, and action to guide you." There was a momentary silence. "And remember that not all of the people who have hurt you did so deliberately. Some of them are just careless, or self-absorbed, or didn't know better. Some of them can't escape the negativity around them."

"I think…that makes sense."

"These ideas have been with us since the beginning, with all humans, but they get buried by everyday human experiences, by the illusion of the world outside, by temptation, by greed, by the very nature of who we are as humans," the monk continued.

"That sounds like what I learned in Bible lessons as a kid."

"So now you have to re-learn these ideas, re-discover these ideas, but they have always been with you, somewhere," he said.

"They have?" she asked, then nodded and said, "You're right, they have."

"Go and rest now," he said. "Remember that to help yourself, or help others, you need to strive for higher values. When you do that, your lower quality values and feelings and emotions will be replaced by higher, more positive emotions. Don't ever give in to your negative emotions."

"But is there something I can do immediately to get rid of these negative feelings?" Maya asked.

"Focus on service, Maya, and higher ideals. That will replace these negative feelings that you feel, the frustration that you feel."

"I've done some community service," Maya said.

The monk cleared his throat again. "I mean intentional service. And I mean an attitude of service, of giving instead of taking."

"An attitude of service. Of giving," she repeated. "Okay, professor. I'll try."

"Think about how much has been given to you for free, that people take for granted. Have gratitude for that. Set your mind on a higher interest, see beyond your little world. Cultivate an attitude of service. Too much of the world is focused on taking, on extraction for personal gain."

"Okay. I think I understand."

"Your actions now sow the seeds of the future, so take the right actions," he said. "The past is the past. You don't have to let your past affect you, but you can choose how you respond in the future, with the knowledge you have gained from past experiences."

"Is it really that simple?" Maya asked, dumbfounded.

"It can be, if you focus on what you can do now, on moving

forward. It's your choice. The path forward may be lonely at times, but it's the only way."

"So what do I do now?" Maya asked. "What's the first step?"

"You must choose to develop your inner strength now, to be self-sufficient, so that you do not get frustrated by the realities of the world. You must find your purpose and find what brings meaning to you."

"I don't understand how to do that, though!"

"People usually feel disappointment when their expectations are not met. When there is a mismatch between reality and expectations, people feel stressed, frustrated, agitated. They do not realize that there is a nature to the creatures and things around them in the world, and to humans."

"But how does that matter?"

"It matters because it is difficult to change the nature of most things in the world, but people do have the ability to change their nature, by learning, studying, reflecting, and having intention," the monk said.

"But what about the people stuck in war?"

"That is not your situation. You are not stuck. So, you need to decide what your role is going to be, and then put your effort into that role."

"But is that enough?" Maya asked.

"You cannot get obsessed with the results. Just keep focusing on the actions you take, and take them consistently, and with genuine gratitude and intent and effort, Maya."

Maya hesitated. Somehow it didn't feel like that would be enough. "Will I ever be able to speak to you again?"

There was a pause. "It's likely."

"I never said thank you all these years when we've spoken. And I only know you as the professor," Maya said. "I've never even known your real name."

There was a long silence, then he responded, "I am known by the name Tsenzhab."

PART FIVE

"We must let go of the life we have planned, so as to accept the one that is waiting for us."
—*Joseph Campbell*

PERSPECTIVE

Maya became accustomed to meditating on the words that Tsenzhab had shared with her. She would wake early in the morning before classes and sit on the floor of her studio, cross her legs, put her arms on her knees, and close her eyes. As she did this, she tried to remember the spirit of what he had said to her. She reminded herself that she needed to be okay doing her part to help others while continuing to move forward with her own life. She reminded herself that she needed to learn to be at peace, despite whatever frustrations and failures and betrayals she faced. She knew she needed to accept what she had learned through Vik's betrayal, the government's betrayals, her father's kidnapping, and Jeev's and even Mrs. Fernandes' betrayals. She knew she could not get hung up on all of that, and that she needed to try to recognize their humanity. This would be the only way she could move forward.

#

As she was becoming more accustomed to her new routines, Maya often thought of Kelsie and what a true friend she was, as well as how well-adjusted Kelsie had always seemed.

"How did you do it, Kels?" Maya asked her one evening from the phone booth on her floor. "How were you okay right from the start?"

"I don't know. I haven't been through anything like what you've been through… Sure, I've had my moments of self-doubt, and even gender discrimination, but I had my parents reassuring me the whole way through, helping me work through those moments."

"Your mom is really great," Maya said.

"I feel like we're all just spending too much time worrying about external validation. I learned early not to worry about that," Kelsie said. "I'm really grateful to my mom for that lesson."

"Yeah, people do things that don't make sense. And sometimes we just need to stand up for what is right, regardless of the consequence."

"It's hard. I know, Maya."

"You never did tell me the details about your trip to Norway."

"I really want to find time to go back and volunteer with the NGO, or even find a permanent job with them. I really admire what they're doing. They've often been the first organization to step in and help with various crises around the world."

"Wow. That takes courage."

"What about you?"

"I'm starting to feel better. Maybe I failed in my efforts to address the injustices I saw, but I'm trying to be okay with that," Maya said.

"You can't beat yourself up too much over that. There's only so much one person can do," Kelsie said.

"I know. You're right. I'm finally accepting that."

#

"Instead of taking from the world, give," Tsenzhab said to Maya when they next spoke. "True love is unconditional. It does not require someone giving you something in exchange. The state

PERSPECTIVE

of love for most humans, right now, is closer to the concept of attachment, like a two-way transaction. When love is polluted by selfishness, it is attachment. Practice removing your selfishness. True love is unconditional. We should love and care for our fellow humans unconditionally. Though, as one person, you must decide where your purpose and obligations lie, and focus on that."

As the fall semester got underway, Maya tried to remain focused on the positive thoughts she was putting inside her head, the habits she was developing, and on what Tsenzhab had advised. Although at times Maya still questioned what she should do, she was relieved not to find her thoughts drifting to the drug store anymore.

Tsenzhab had advised that the rioting, the targeted kidnappings and killings, and what seemed like ethnic cleansing, was ultimately all driven by human ego and selfishness. She still could not fathom, though, what drove Jeev's cruelty, although it was becoming clearer that his father's antagonism had played some sort of role in shaping how Jeev interacted with the world.

Maya remembered a friend of her aunt Rosie whom she and her father had visited on that first trip back to Sri Lanka in 1983. The man was a doctor and spent all of his waking hours with patients. His family had become angry with him because his focus on his patients caused him to miss family functions and gatherings. His family thought he was callous at first, but then came to learn that he had woken up to his calling in life and had chosen to really dedicate himself to it.

Maya remembered visiting him in his bachelor's apartment on the hospital grounds with her father. He had been so busy but had left his shift to come and greet them and show them around the hospital grounds.

"I'm trying to be objective and help anyone who is hurt, injured, or ill, and not get caught up in the emotions and hatred that can come from the government's transgressions," he'd explained.

Maya recognized now that he was trying to turn this negative energy into positive work and thought about how challenging that must have been under the circumstances. He became a role model to Maya, who realized she needed to develop real and objective focus like that.

#

As the semester progressed, Maya started to become more productive. She concentrated more on really listening to and learning from her colleagues and her students, less on being worried about the people around her. She began to get out of bed every day feeling a sense of purpose that was not weighed down by guilt or frustration, even though the situation in Sri Lanka continued to worsen and some news outlets were saying that over a hundred thousand people had been displaced and were living as refugees in nearby countries like India.

That December, when Maya was restless again, it was not borne of frustration. It was borne of a sense of purpose and service. She had learned of an organization in South India that had begun helping war refugees through housing and economic development efforts, as well as providing health and mental health counseling. As they were in desperate need of volunteers, Maya decided she would go there to help.

Maya had already been trained on triage-level mental health counseling, thanks to Sister Lucy and the peer counseling and crisis hotline all those years ago. Her father also went through a triage training course that several volunteer doctors had set up to prepare volunteers who were going to work temporarily in the war refugee camps.

"It's ironic, isn't it, Maya? Now I, too, am trained as a triage counselor and mental health counselor, like you," her father said when she was home for a weekend. "I've learned how to recognize post-traumatic stress disorder, depression, anxiety, and how to speak with the refugees who might seek mental health counseling."

Maya and her father were also going to be given the opportunity to go on health triage visits and learn first-hand about the health and mental health issues that the refugees were facing every day. She also was going to meet with the economic development consultants there who were managing microcredit loans to help the more entrepreneurial refugees create a living to supplement the government relief payments. They would be taken around to different refugee camps to learn about the various cottage industries that people had set up, ranging from building chicken coops to harvesting eggs to weaving textiles.

When Maya called Kelsie to share her news, Kelsie in turn shared that she would be spending her winter break in Norway. Her parents had saved up money and given her the trip as a holiday gift. She was going to apply for a job with the Norwegian NGO.

BECAUSE OF WAR

After an uneventful flight to India, Maya and her father arrived at their hostel in the state of Tamil Nadu in the southern part of the country, where they would be hosted for the duration of their volunteer work.

"Don't be nervous for the hostel, Maya. We just can't stay in a normal hotel while we work with people in refugee camps, right?" her father said to her as they entered the lobby.

The lobby was plain with white walls. There were a few old chairs and a television set on a table covered with a simple madras print tablecloth. There was a pungent smell of curry leaf and chilis and lentils and idlis wafting through the air, and Maya inhaled deeply. It reminded her of grandmother's house in Sri Lanka.

"Breakfast is served from seven o'clock in the morning, sir," the man at the reception desk was telling her father. "There will be extra bottles of cleaned and filtered water available at breakfast."

This was going to be a new challenge for Maya. When she was little, on a few occasions, her father had taken care of looking out for what she and her brothers ate and drank, making sure that no contaminated food or water came onto their plates or into their cups. Now, in India, where water safety was different, Maya had to look out for herself and remember to be careful to eat only cooked food and drink only filtered or newly bottled water.

"Let me take you up to your room, sir," the man at the reception desk said. When he came out from behind his desk, Maya saw that he was much shorter than she'd thought. He was wearing a white collared button-down shirt, polyester gray pants, and brown sandals. He had a dark mustache and his hair had been oiled back. Maya was not surprised that he was constantly addressing her father instead of her; she would need to re-adjust to the male-dominated environment she was in and be okay with it if she was going to focus properly on the volunteer work she had come here to do.

"No, it's okay, we can carry them ourselves," her father said as the man lifted their suitcases. "Just lead the way."

The staircase was narrow, with windows on each landing, and they walked up three flights before the man opened a large brown door.

Maya followed them into the room. It was plain and bare. There were simple twin beds with white sheets underneath a window, and by the door there was a closet with sliding doors. There also was an old built-in cabinet in between the closet and door with the paint chipping off of it.

"Here is the bathroom also," the man said as he went out into the hallway and opened the bathroom door, inviting them to come and view it.

Maya peered inside. The bathroom was plain and white and simple, just the basics. She was surprised to see a small plastic shower curtain, and relieved to see the western-style shower and western-style toilet to which she was accustomed. She had worried they would have to use the traditional toilet, a cemented hole in the ground.

Before the man took his leave, he said, "Remember that if you have any laundry, just bring it down to the front desk during the mornings. It will get washed within two or three days and then brought back to you."

Maya's father thanked him, then shut the door and started unpacking some of his papers from his smaller personal bag.

"What's that?" Maya asked.

"Those are the reference sheets from the triage training program. I wanted to review them today before we go to the first refugee camp tomorrow. I'm not as familiar with these things as you are."

#

Later that day, before dinner, a brown van came to pick up Maya and Oliver. They were going to be taken to meet the man who had been managing some of the work related to the refugee camps.

Maya looked out of the window of the van at the crowded streets. There were cars and scooters and auto-rickshaws and bicycles and pedestrians rushing around on the road in disparate directions, and it was loud and dusty. The scooters made drill-like sounds and there were so many that the noise of them often overpowered the honking cars.

After what felt like a long time in the chaotic traffic, they arrived and the van parked next to an old building. They walked up a short staircase and entered a disorganized room that was being used as an office.

"Welcome, welcome." A man with glasses and gray hair and white cotton shirt extended his hand to Maya's father. He took her father's hands with his right hand and laid his left hand on top. "Welcome, I'm glad you could make it."

The man sat down at his desk on an old black plastic chair that was falling apart, and Maya's father took the plastic chair next to the man's desk.

"Come, Maya," the man said, pointing to another plastic chair and motioning for Maya to sit.

"Tell us, what is the news?" her father asked.

They continued their conversation for the next thirty minutes, prepping for their visit to the first refugee camp the next day.

#

They were picked up by a van again the next morning and dropped at a gray, concrete, nondescript building at one of the refugee camp sites. It was isolated and dusty there, and the building was run down. They hadn't expected more, as the government in India had designated unused buildings to house the incoming war refugees. It was a two-room building, with desktop computers set up on two rows of folding tables in the main room, and metal folding chairs set up in a circle in the adjoining room. Sunlight poured in through the one window in the main room.

A man arrived and escorted Maya and her father to the adjoining room.

"This is the room we use for counseling. Have a seat here."

"Thank you. When do we see the people who want to be counseled?" Maya's father asked.

"There are two people here now. They were anxious to speak to you."

As the man left the room, Maya's father turned to her and said, "Maybe you can observe me and give me feedback, since you've been doing this longer than me? So, I can do the talking today, if that's ok with you? Then we can reverse it tomorrow."

Maya agreed. She wasn't sure what to expect and was fine with only observing the first day.

A woman and a younger girl were brought in to see them.

"Let's all sit down," Maya's father said.

Maya nodded to acknowledge the woman and the young girl, and then placed her hands on her lap to listen.

"Tell me, why did you come here today?" Maya's father asked.

"I don't have the energy to live anymore," the young girl said in a quiet voice, looking down at her lap. Her mother remained silent.

"Why?" her father asked.

"We did not see this war coming, and were forced to flee our homes," the girl said.

"Yes…" Maya's father said solemnly. "Then tell me about school."

The young girl shrugged her shoulders, keeping her eyes focused on her bare feet on the concrete floor. She was fidgeting nervously, twisting her hands and pulling out the creases in her pants. She was dressed in a woman's long yellow cotton shirt and pajama pants, cool on those hot sticky days in the refugee camp, but not something she would ordinarily wear, Maya knew.

Maya's father shifted his look to the girl's mother, but she remained silent. He wiped beads of perspiration off his forehead with a handkerchief, and then folded it back into a triangular formation and stuffed it back in his pocket.

"How about it, how is school?" Maya's father asked again.

"It's fine, I suppose," the girl said, looking up to his chest-level and smiling awkwardly.

Maya noticed that she made no eye contact with her mother, and that her mother made no eye contact with her, and that worried her. Maya had heard that suicide levels were up in the refugee camps, and that the causes were numerous and varied. Many people simply couldn't cope with the stress of moving to a new land, the different way people lived, the pollution and crowding, the living conditions and lack of privacy, and the general loss of free will. Jobs were scarce, too, and support was not available to all those who could not procure jobs. Some people were also barred from accessing the high school or college level education, for fear of overcrowding. Women had been raped during attacks back in

Sri Lanka and had never received any treatment for that, nor the opportunity to recover properly, and they carried those traumatic memories with them into the refugee camps.

Maya knew her father just needed to identify this girl's reason for loss of interest in life. Then he could recommend the appropriate follow-up therapy to the doctors who would visit the refugee camps, and they could work with the girl through her distress.

"You know, you are very lucky to be able to attend school," Maya's father said to the girl. "Tell me, who do you spend time with at school?"

There was a long silence. The girl continued to twist her fingers. "I…uhhh…," she started. "I enjoy the free time between classes."

"But who do you spend time with at school? Tell him. That is what he wants to know," the mother urged.

The young girl let out a sigh. "The girls are all very nice at school, but…"

"Yes, that's good. But what?" Maya's father asked gently.

"What do we all have to look forward to? I go to school every day. I sit in the classroom that we built. We talk to the teacher and to the other students. And then we walk home and tend to our chores, and eat dinner in one room together, and sleep in the same room together. Then we get up the next day and do the same. Every day it is the same. What else is there for us?"

Having poured out all her thoughts at once, the girl looked down at her lap. And there it sat in the bare room, the truth, her truth, as cool as the breeze that had passed through minutes before.

"I cannot bear it anymore," the girl blurted out. "I can't even spend time with who I want to spend time with."

"How so?" Maya's father asked.

"There's…there's a boy," the girl said.

"A boy?"

"Yes. We love each other, but…"

"I understand," Maya's father reassured her.

Maya opened the satchel she had brought with her and handed her father the reference sheet. It was where the other doctors' information was. She knew her father would have to refer this case both to the volunteer general practice physician there, as well as the volunteer psychiatrist. This girl would have to be examined for possible physical violations, as well as treated for her depression.

#

Maya and her father went back every day for a week. On the last two days, Maya was shown the cottage industries that refugees had taken up with the microcredit loans. When she returned back to the hostel, Maya put pen to paper in the evening. She had been told by Sister Lucy that penning her thoughts and observations on her experience in the refugee camps could be helpful to some of the organizations that Sister Lucy knew of through her church. They would be able to use the firsthand experience and observations as a primary source for any training they might do for volunteers at those same refugee camps, or in Sri Lanka. So Maya tried to capture her observations as honestly as she could. She began writing.

> *During my journey, I had the chance to spend some time volunteering with a health and economic development organization within a refugee camp in Asia. I jumped at this opportunity to learn and observe how humans operate and thrive in less than ideal and highly pressured environments.*
>
> *This organization also set up health clinics for civil war refugees from within Asia. I spent several weeks traveling between refugee camps, observing, learning, and interviewing. Each camp*

was different, influenced by its immediate geography and environmental conditions. Housing facilities varied, but often entire families shared just one room. Sanitation facilities and areas for getting rid of human waste also varied, as did the presence and quality of the makeshift health clinics and schools. In summary, most facilities were poor, dirty, run down, and unsanitary.

However, I was struck by the spirit of the people living in these camps. I was struck by their smiles. By their banter. By the community they offered one another. It was as if they did not see the poverty, the dirt, the rundown facilities, their cramped spaces, and the unsanitary conditions. Many of them came from second-to-third world facilities when they fled civil war, but the refugee camps might have been considered fourth world.

The children eagerly attend school every day, sometimes sitting on the dirt ground under nothing more than a sheet spread out over two sticks to block the sun, and at other times in makeshift buildings that have been constructed for the purpose of being a large, multi-purpose classroom. They learn their ABC's, their math, songs to sing, and more. They were eager to be there. Many have dreams of making it to college. This simple essay cannot describe how hopeful and eager they were, despite their circumstances.

The adults in the community found or created work where they could. Some had the opportunity to start small chicken farms. Others started tailoring businesses. Cottage industry entrepreneurship and business ownership was a dream several women and men pursued. They were given the chance to take out microloans to fund their ventures and were given support and business counseling.

As I reflect on this experience, I cannot help but admire their persistence and their relentless pursuit to create opportunity for themselves and the communities around them. The people in these communities taught me five lessons about the key traits that are important in sustaining efforts and thriving: resourcefulness, *effort and work ethic, persistence, attitude, and the ability to tap networks.*

Resourcefulness came as a natural outgrowth of the shortages of resources. Resourcefulness was creativity in development, production, and management of everything from redesigning their living and workspaces to creating meeting rooms and schools to organizing makeshift health clinics to refurbishing computers and batteries, despite a lack of funding for resources. It was inspired by discomfort and a desire to strive for something better for themselves and for those around them.

Their effort and work ethic were consistent and continuous. Effort was their self-propelled education in continuous improvement, and their daily routine, ensuring they were present when opportunity presented itself. It came from a work ethic that valued consistency and productivity regardless of circumstances. In addition, the people in the camps had become attuned to those things they could and could not control, and focused their efforts on those they could.

They persisted. Persistence was never giving up, regardless of circumstances or the availability of support and resources. It was focused adherence to a goal greater than oneself. Those that survived their circumstances had something in common - they never gave up trying. They lived to keep trying. They were committed to the relentless pursuit of opportunity both for themselves and the communities around them.

Attitude was the most important decision they made day-to-day. As humans we have the choice to determine and to control our attitude. How a person chooses to perceive and to react to a situation, whether bad or good, can allow that person to survive a dire situation, and ultimately learn from it. The attitude and spirit of the adults and children alike were hopeful and eager. They chose to take what they had been given, to be grateful, and to work every day to improve the situation of the communities around them.

> *The people there tapped their fellow community members and networks to provide the support and camaraderie they needed to survive. Those networks were the great sounding boards and interfaces that helped move thoughts and ideas forward. Their networks were harnessed intelligently and therefore were more powerful than any one element in the network alone, and so they accomplished more things together.*
>
> *I remain in awe of what I learned on this trip. I remain in awe of the people I met. It has reinforced my enduring belief in the power of human drive and will to improve lives and communities.*

Maya put her pen down and re-read what she had written. There was no doubt she had been fortunate to meet such a hopeful and generous group of people. She was humbled by how much she could learn from people who had so much less than her, and whose futures were much less certain than hers. She knew that the time she and others had spent volunteering was not enough to move the needle on enabling them to leave the refugee camps; they had been displaced and no government was yet willing to grant them asylum and citizenship. They had only been given a temporary home, and they had made the best of it.

#

Something surprising happened when Maya returned back to the US. Other members of the community, people her father knew and friends and relatives, learned of what Maya and her father had tried to do in the refugee camps, and what other volunteers before them had done to support the triage efforts there. There was an unexpected outpouring of letters from people sharing stories of what they themselves had been through, what struggles they had met over the years. Maya read each of them with curiosity and humility, with a yearning to learn and understand.

Maya also learned of a series of massacres that had occurred in December in Sri Lanka, killing hundreds of innocent Tamil civilians. The government army, and in some cases civilian mobs, had entered at least five or six different villages and massacred families in cold blood. Some were rounded up and shot, while others were burned alive in their own residences. Women were raped. The freedom fighting groups were continuing their retaliatory acts, as well, and over the past year and a half, had engaged in attacks on both military and civilians. The war was raging on.

HIM

Maya saw him one morning at a corner near campus, a few days after the middle of January, as she was waiting to cross the street. At least she thought it was Jase. She had not seen him in months.

The light turned green and Maya quickly crossed, with both hands holding tight to her bag, which was slung across her shoulders. It *was* Jase. Seeing him caused her both pleasure and pain, but Maya put aside her ego and waved and called out, "Jase!"

Jase stopped and turned around. Everything about him evoked a sense of familiar warmth—his confident smile, his straight brownish-blond hair, his sharp nose and cheekbones, his liquid blue eyes. He was wearing blue jeans and a button-down shirt and a brown suede jacket and was more handsome than ever.

He waited until Maya got close enough that he could reach out and grab her shoulders.

"It's you, Maya," he said, with a huge smile. "I've been looking for you."

"You were looking for me? Why?" Maya asked.

"Look, you must hate me. I know it's been months," Jase said. "Is there somewhere we can go to talk?"

Maya thought about the sense of generosity she had discussed with Tsenzhab.

"I'm just heading to my last class. We still have an exam that was scheduled after the holidays for some reason," Maya said, with a flurry of excitement coursing through her. "Why don't you come with me to my class, and then we can go somewhere after that to talk?"

"Okay, lead the way," Jase said.

They reached the classroom and entered through the side door, then snaked their way down the right aisle and over a few backpacks. They came to two empty seats and sat down. Maya placed her bag on the floor and pulled out her notebook and pen.

"I hope you don't mind, but I need to pay attention here." It felt great to have Jase next to her again, his shoulders nearly pressed against hers. She had forgotten how sturdy he was, and how good he smelled. It was going to be hard for Maya to fully focus on the lecture.

Sixty minutes later, the classroom buzzed as students chatted while putting their notes away and standing up from their seats.

"Where to now?" Jase asked.

"Let's go to the coffee shop near here, just a few blocks. We can talk there," Maya said, sliding her notebook back in her bag.

As they exited the building and started toward the coffee shop, their strides in step with each other, Maya said, "Soooo… are you going to make me ask?"

"Ask what?"

"Why are you here? And why haven't I heard from you in such a long time?" Maya said, trying not to sound hurt.

Jase was quiet for a minute, then said, "Well, it's funny, really. You know my company was trying to transfer me permanently out to Texas, right? Or maybe you didn't know that."

"Maybe I knew. I don't remember."

"I've been working out of Texas for a few months."

"Oh. Is that why I hadn't heard from you?"

Jase exhaled, turning to look at Maya. "I'm so sorry, Maya. I should've called. But I couldn't deal with the idea that I could have lost you when you went back… I guess I was trying to protect myself."

Maya looked at him in disbelief.

"But I missed you," Jase said quickly.

"Then why didn't you call?" Maya asked.

"I don't know, but I kept coming back to something in my head every day that I was out there."

"What's that?" Maya asked.

"That something was missing in my life."

Jase stopped walking and so did Maya.

"Being away from you got me thinking…about us," Jase said. "I've been a fool, Maya. I've never met anyone like you. I liked you back in high school, and now, well, it's a lot more than that."

Maya didn't respond.

"I knew I had to come back for you, and see if you'd still have me," Jase said.

Maya relented. She wasn't going to let her hurt feelings get in the way of their relationship. Jase had his reasons for doing what he did, and she had her reasons for forgiving him.

"I'm touched, Jase."

Jase smiled. "I know you need to be here for a few more years, for your teaching position and your graduate work."

"I do."

"So, the bottom line is, I think I'm going to turn down my company's offer to transfer out to Texas."

"But didn't you tell me that the position out there was a better management track position?"

"Yes. But I can wait for another opportunity, or even switch companies if I need to."

"You can?" Maya asked. She felt a bittersweet euphoria listening to everything he was saying, and she wanted to savor the moment, the gentle sound of his voice, the soft look on his face, the anticipation of what might come next. She took it all in. She looked at Jase and nodded, to signal she was still listening.

"How would you feel if I stayed here in Pennsylvania? If you can forgive me, that is," Jase asked.

Maya was both thrilled and terrified by the weight of what Jase was suggesting, but she quickly resolved to shove her fear aside. "I would really like that," she said.

"You would?"

"Yes. I mean, I wouldn't want you to sacrifice your career, but I really would like that a lot."

"You know, I haven't stopped thinking about you." Jase reached out to grab Maya's hands and clasped them together, held them in his hands, and brought them to his chest.

Maya felt the warmth of Jase's hands and she squeezed them as they started walking again. Her mind was whirling with this turn of events, and she felt so inexperienced that she truly wasn't sure how much she should wear her heart on her sleeve. This was a whole new area of ego and emotion she would need to work through, and right now she didn't know how she would tackle it. So she decided to just be present in the moment. Just because Jase might stay back in Pennsylvania for work didn't necessarily mean they would continue to be together for the long-term, but she hoped that they might.

When they got to the crowded coffee shop, Jase went up to order and Maya searched for an empty table. She found two stools at the long bar along the windows overlooking the street and put some napkins down on the seat beside her to keep it.

Within a few minutes, Jase came over with two bottled waters and a muffin. "Here you go." Maya removed the napkins from the empty stool and Jase sat down.

"So, what have you been doing these past couple of months?" Jase asked.

It was a far more loaded question than Jase realized, and Maya knew she'd fill him in eventually. For now she just said, "A lot. So much. I'll tell you all about it another time."

"Tell me now. Why not?"

Maya contemplated what he said. Jase was right. If they were turning a new leaf in their relationship, she had to be able to trust him fully and confide in him, so why not start now?

"Where to begin? I'm good now, but there were some rough times," Maya said. "I've been figuring a lot of things out."

"About?" Jase asked.

"About things that happened, and about myself. I never did really tell you about everything that happened in July two summers ago."

"No, you didn't."

"Yeah. I'm okay now, but there are a lot of people that weren't okay, that were killed. It was really horrible to witness," Maya said. "Now I'm really focused on seeing what I can do to help, and I'm a lot less frustrated by the constant hurdles and disappointments."

"That's comforting to hear. You *do* seem different now. Calmer," Jase said, putting his hand tenderly on Maya's hands.

"I really felt lost sometimes, but now it's much better."

Jase caressed Maya's hands. "You know you can tell me anything, Maya. I want to hear what you have to say."

So Maya talked. She told Jase what it had been like to come to America in her early days, and she told him about the horrors she had experienced that fateful July, and she told him about the trip back to Sri Lanka and her father's kidnapping and the disappointment she had felt in not being able to help extricate others. Then she told him about going to India in December to work with displaced families.

"My God, Maya, I didn't know," Jase said, stroking Maya's

shoulder and upper arm. "I'm such an ass for not writing or calling. That must have been beyond difficult. Can you ever forgive me?"

"I think I can," she said instinctively, and smiled at him.

Jase cleared his throat and said, "You made it home. I'm glad you made it back or we wouldn't have had a chance to reconnect again."

"I'm glad we reconnected, too," Maya said, feeling herself getting lost in Jase's eyes.

"I'm glad you made it through."

"Yeah, thanks to the silent heroes in my life."

"Silent heroes?"

"Like Sister Lucy and Kelsie, and this professor Sister Lucy introduced to me who used to be a monk. His name is Tsenzhab and he's shared a lot of wisdom with me."

Jase sat quietly listening, keeping his hand on Maya's.

"Why didn't you tell me any of this earlier?" Then a look of recognition softened Jase's eyes. "I know I made that impossible the last few months, but did you think you couldn't tell me before?"

"I think I was ashamed of feeling helpless and frustrated and disheartened before I learned to stand on my own feet."

Jase nodded. "Well look, we're a team now, and teams get more done together."

There was silence as they both took a sip of water from their water bottles.

Jase looked at Maya. "Well, at least we have more time together to look forward to, right?" he said in his usual upbeat tone. "Since I'm not going to Texas, I need to figure out what's going to make sense for me long-term. I want to do something where I can look at myself in the mirror every morning and be proud of what I've done."

"I understand."

Jase looked at his watch. "It's getting late. Maybe we can meet tomorrow? Or maybe after your exams?" he suggested.

"That would be great."

Jase leaned over and kissed Maya on her cheek. Then he moved toward her mouth and kissed her tenderly again. "I missed you," he said.

They said their goodbyes and hugged. Maya walked out of the coffee shop, unabashedly ecstatic. She knew she just had to get these last few exams behind her, and then she would be done with her semester and could really bask in the excitement of how she and Jase had left things. She finally felt mature enough to have the relationship with Jase she really wanted to have, because she finally respected herself.

LETTER

Even though she had plummeted close to the very depths that any human could go, Maya had somehow made it out okay, and she felt a great deal of gratitude for this. She realized she could begin to forgive some of the people that had hurt her—that she *had* to forgive them, because she understood now about the nature of humans, about the nature of the world. She could not hold on to anger or disappointment. It was too destructive. It was counterproductive.

Her second semester teaching had come to a close and Maya went on a search to find both Sister Lucy and Tsenzhab. She wanted to thank Sister Lucy for contacting the organizations she knew on the ground—the church groups and other local humanitarian charities—and she found her, as expected, at the office of the crisis hotline. After a long and earnest conversation, Maya went back to campus to find Tsenzhab.

She had to thank Tsenzhab for the profound wisdom he had shared with her. Maya had planned on visiting him at some point in the next few days, but she felt a sense of urgency now because Sister Lucy had shared that Tsenzhab was ill.

Maya rapped on the glass panel of the door to his office and waited for a response.

"Professor?" she called after a few minutes.

She knocked harder on the glass panel.

"Professor?"

Maya smelled something strange. She knocked again and then opened the door. A man was on the floor grabbing at his chest and smoke was emanating from an incense holder on the table next to him.

"Professor? What's going on? Can I help?" Maya asked.

"There, in my jacket," he gasped, pointing to a jacket on a wall hook.

"What happened?" Maya asked, grabbing the jacket.

"I have finished…"

"Finished? Finished what?"

"My job."

"Let me call 911."

"Forgiveness…"

"It's me, Maya, Professor. I came here to thank you. Please, stay still, I'm calling for help."

"Forgiveness, Maya," he said, wheezing. "Without ego. Don't forget…"

Maya found the phone under a pile of papers on the professor's desk and dialed 911. "Come quickly, please!" she said, giving the address of the building to the dispatcher.

"There is nothing…"

"Yes?" Maya said, dropping the phone and kneeling next to the professor.

"Nothing unsaid…or undone."

"To whom?" Maya asked, confused.

"To…you," he whispered.

"Me?"

The professor looked at Maya. His eyes were closing and she didn't know what to do, how to comfort him. Or why the ambulance was taking so long to arrive.

"Professor?" Maya said, putting her hand on his cheek. "Hold on, please! The ambulance is coming," Maya pleaded.

"I have shared…the truth…with you…"

"Wait, please, they are coming," Maya said again. She grabbed his head. "Stay awake, please. Help is coming."

"Take this knowledge with you…"

"Please, stay with me, they are almost here," Maya said as tears rolled down her cheeks.

"Share it…"

The professor seemed to collapse into himself. There was nothing Maya could do. She just sat there feeling helpless and numb, holding his head until the medics arrived.

#

Maya looked down at the letter in her hands before placing it on the desk in her studio. The return address was Pennsylvania, but she didn't recognize the sender's name. She wasn't quite sure why she felt so nervous, although sometimes she still received letters from people about their experiences as refugees, and each one tore at her heart. Recently she'd learned that another library in the northern part of Sri Lanka, not too far from her grandmother's home, had been bombed after dozens of people had been rounded up and lured there, and everyone within its walls had died.

The letter could also be an update on Jeev, who had visited Sri Lanka himself a few months earlier and then gone missing. Some suspected he had been kidnapped, and despite what he'd done to her, Maya only thought of him with compassion and hoped for his safe return.

Holding the letter with two hands, Maya tore it open with one of her fingernails and pulled out a folded, crisp white page full of scratchy blue handwriting.

The letter was from one of the women Maya knew from the

crisis hotline. She was sorry to write, the woman said, but she knew Maya would want to know that Sister Lucy had passed.

Maya's heart seized. She truly loved Sister Lucy and had just seen her weeks ago, just before she had seen Tsenzhab.

Sister Lucy had taught her to be okay with herself, to forgive herself, to pick up the pieces and move forward from her mistakes. Sister Lucy had been the embodiment of compassion and acceptance and unselfish love. She had always been so focused on giving to others that she didn't have time to worry about what might be missing in her own life. She had chosen a life dedicated toward loving, caring for, and supporting other people.

Maya thought back to all of those letters she had written to Sister Lucy while she was away during college, and the letter she had written just a few months ago but never mailed. She had been too embarrassed to send that one, that last one. Why hadn't she sent that last letter out?

Maya went to her closet and found her memory box sitting on the shelf above her clothes rack. She reached for it and pulled it down. The old wooden box had moved with Maya everywhere, during her childhood and college, and now to her studio.

She opened the box and rummaged through the items in it and found the letter to Sister Lucy.

> *Dear Sister Lucy,*
>
> *There is so much I have yearned to tell you, so much I want to share with you now. How I wish I had shared it with you before, but I was like a memory box that had lost its key, and I didn't know how to begin, how to find my voice and speak to you about all of this.*
>
> *You were my source of solace on the other end of the phone, all those months ago, when I was contemplating the unspeakable because I was in the depths of despair. You listened to me and*

gave me counsel, and so I need to write this to you. I need to tell you this story.

I have never felt fully free from my past, uncuffed, until now. I was especially distressed, feeling trapped, after experiencing what people are now calling Black July. But even before that, I struggled to find my place in the world. It was challenging to process everything that was going on in my life, and I was ashamed at times for my inability to just be happy and leave everything unpleasant in the past.

But something started to happen to me last summer, a transformation that gave me a new and permanent perspective on my past. I began to pick up wisdom from others who knew more than me, like you and Tsenzhab, but it took a while for it to fully sink in. And it's still very much a journey that is unfolding for me.

My life has shifted 180 degrees. I have been awakened. I have been working toward having things more under control now - my perceptions, my actions - and I hope this hard-won clarity does not disappear. Now I can try to dedicate my life to my true purpose.

I know there won't be easy or fast solutions. I know that people aren't going to come running to help immediately. I figured out that I just have to do my part, despite how frustrating the journey can be.

I can't help but reflect now on the lessons I learned along the way from the vagaries of my life, especially these past few years, some of which came from your example and kindness:

I learned it's important to cultivate gratitude for life, home, family, and friends; that home is a concept, not a place; and that we can find glorious friends and good people, even in new places.

I learned that the stories we fabricate in our minds, that we tell ourselves, matter, because they conjure our realities, so we must choose them carefully.

I learned we should not be too hard on ourselves, or weighed down by expectations; that we need to move on, and not let tumultuous experiences define us or anchor us.

I learned that it's important to be kind, to speak positively, take time to laugh, and be light-hearted.

I learned that people are only human, so we need to learn to depend on ourselves, keep our own counsel and not wait for external validation.

And I learned that a few people will surprise us, because heroes come in surprising shapes and sizes and colors.

Yours,
Maya

ACKNOWLEDGMENTS

A number of primary sources and secondary sources were consulted before and during the development of this work of fiction. I want to acknowledge these sources of information. While not an exhaustive list, some examples include *Vedanta Treatise* by A. Parthasarathy, *Meditations* by Marcus Aurelius, *The Enchiridion* by Epictetus, *The Bhagavad Gita* translated by Barbara Stoler Miller, *Buddhist Scriptures* as represented by Donald S. Lopez, Jr., *The Power of Now* by Eckhart Tolle, Catholic Relief Services, Amnesty International, The International Commission of Jurists, The Centre for Poverty Analysis, Tamil Centre for Human Rights, OfERR, Sciences Po, BBC News, Tamil Guardian, The Economist, Daily Mirror (Sri Lanka).

I want to thank the following people who helped make this novel possible. They include Corey Stewart, Gordon McClellan and his entire team, Michiko Clark, Laurence O'Bryan, Anand, Adam, Ken, Michael Neff, Paula Munier.

I also want to thank Ritika and Gautam Jain, Sr Donna, Sr Sandy, Sr Ernestine, and Sam for the invaluable work they have performed in various parts of the world.

ABOUT THE AUTHOR

Allie Nava is an American writer who survived the violent anti-minority massacres of 1970s Sri Lanka. Her writing explores the nature of reality, perception, and beliefs, as well as our ability to shape them to live more positive lives. *July and Everything After* is her first novel and previously her short fiction was selected for various literary journals including the award-winning *Six Sentences*. A former executive and editor/writing advisor, she's been a board member or advocate for several mission-oriented organizations including Bellevue Literary Review and Golden Seeds, and has been recognized for her work by several organizations including Amazon, Harvard, and Asia Society. You can find her online at www.allienava.com.

Printed in Great Britain
by Amazon

6629de5e-9c6e-48cc-b4df-ad416a51df44R01